Emilio

TITLES IN THIS SERIES

THROUGH MY EYES
series editor Lyn White

Emilio

SOPHIE MASSON

ALLEN&UNWIN
SYDNEY·MELBOURNE·AUCKLAND·LONDON

This project has been assisted by the Australian Government through the Australia Council, its arts funding and advisory body.

Australian Government

Australia Council for the Arts

A portion of the proceeds (up to $5000) from sales of this series will be donated to UNICEF. UNICEF works in over 190 countries, including those in which books in this series are set, to promote and protect the rights of children. www.unicef.org.au

First published in 2014
Text © Sophie Masson 2014
Series concept © series creator and series editor Lyn White 2014

Allen & Unwin
83 Alexander Street
Crows Nest NSW 2065
Australia
Phone: (61 2) 8425 0100
Email: info@allenandunwin.com
Web: www.allenandunwin.com

A Cataloguing-in-Publication entry is available from the National Library of Australia – www.trove.nla.gov.au

ISBN 978 1 74331 247 6

Teaching and learning guide available from www.allenandunwin.com

Cover and text design by Bruno Herfst and Vincent Agostino
Cover photos from Getty Images and Vicky Kasala (top),
    Chico Sanchez (bottom)
Map of Mexico by Guy Holt
Set in 10.5 pt Plantin by Midland Typesetters, Australia
This book was printed in April 2014 at McPherson's Printing Group,
76 Nelson St, Maryborough, Victoria 3465, Australia.
www.mcphersonsprinting.com.au

10 9 8 7 6 5 4 3 2 1

MIX
Paper from responsible sources
FSC® C001695

The paper in this book is FSC certified. FSC promotes environmentally responsible, socially beneficial and economically viable management of the world's forests.

For Xavier, who helped me feel Mexico

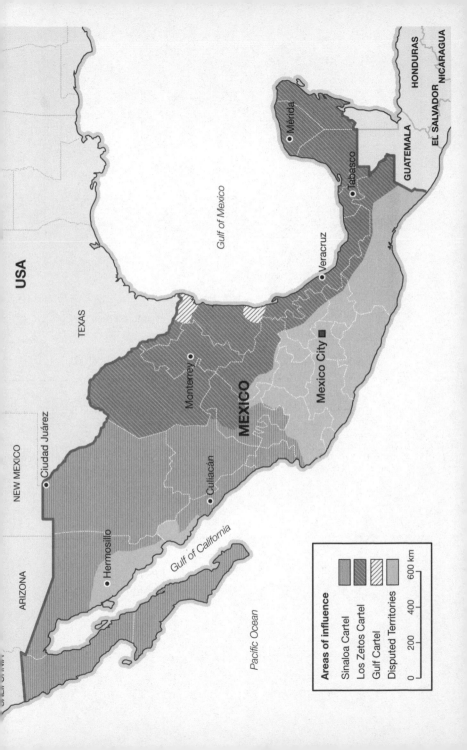

Chapter 1

'**Hey, Emilio,' hissed Pablo,** leaning over the classroom aisle. 'Come to the beach this weekend?'

Keeping a wary eye on Señora Ramirez, who was writing sums on the board, Emilio whispered back, 'Wish I could. But you know Mamá needs me to help Saturday night.'

That very morning, before going to work, his mother had said, 'I know you'd like to go away on the weekend with your friends. But it means so much to me that you'll be there.'

'Mamá, I wouldn't miss your big night,' he'd told her, 'you know I wouldn't.'

'Thank you, Emilio. Your father would have been so proud of you.'

That had brought a lump to his throat. Three years it had been since the car accident killed his father, and yet at times it felt like yesterday.

'Did you hear what I said, hombre?'

He jerked his attention back to Pablo, who was looking at him curiously. 'What?'

'Esteban's older sister Beatriz,' said Pablo. 'The really hot one. She's going to be there too. Want to change your mind?'

Emilio shook his head, smiling. 'I can't. Besides, she wouldn't look twice at you. She's fifteen!'

'What does that matter—'

'Señor Lopez! Señor Vega!' cut in Señora Ramirez. 'I did not know you were such math geniuses that you didn't need to listen! Perhaps you would like to stay in after school today?'

'No, sorry, excuse us, Maestra,' said both boys hastily. They were lucky the bell rang then, and after the usual shuffling of seats and clatter of desktops the whole class gratefully left.

Pablo and Emilio walked out together, with Nina and Sergio and Sierra, making their way through the usual noisy, cheerful afternoon street bustle of Mexico City, cars honking, street vendors singing their wares, loud music belting out from stores, the appetising smells coming from street hawkers' stalls and the stink of car fumes and drains. Grabbing some grilled fish tacos from a hawker along the way, they all hung out together for a while at Nina's place, only a couple of blocks from school. They sat around in the big living room eating, chatting and laughing, sprawled on bright cushions with the TV going in the background, before Pablo headed off home.

'Lucky him, going to the beach,' said Sergio, draining his coffee. 'We haven't had a proper holiday in ages.'

'Neither have we,' said Emilio. 'Mamá works too hard to take any time off.' He sighed. 'And that's only going

2

to get worse now that American company is joining up with her agency.'

'Hey, but at least you'll be rich,' joked Sergio.

Emilio shrugged. 'In your dreams.' His mother was excited about the linkage between her business, Lopez Travel, and an Arizona-based company, Holiday South, but all he could see was that she'd be spending even more hours at the office. Proud as Emilio was of his mother, he also wished, and not for the first time, that things could be different. That his father could still be here so he didn't have to be the man of the house. That he could be free, like Pablo, to go off for a weekend without feeling guilty.

They'd had the TV on in the background, not paying much notice to it, but now an item of news flashed onto the screen and they fell silent. 'Headless bodies found on roadside,' ran the headline, followed by a shot of uniformed police surrounding some blurry shapes. Sierra made a sharp little sound in her throat. 'It's them again,' she whispered. Nobody asked her what she meant. Everyone in Mexico knew about the drug war, which had already claimed tens of thousands of lives in recent years and spread its tentacles into even the safest district.

Nina got up and turned off the TV. 'Hey, has anyone thought about that geography assignment? It's due soon.'

'Trust you to think of that,' grumbled Emilio, secretly relieved that she had changed the subject.

'Someone's got to remind you,' retorted Nina.

The haunted expression vanished from Sierra's face. 'Lucky we have you then, Nina,' she laughed.

'True enough,' said Sergio, with a sideways look at Nina, who tossed her long, shiny hair and shrugged, as she always did when Sergio tried to compliment her. She could be a real prickly cactus sometimes, Emilio thought.

Emilio finally left his friends at around five and headed home. His mother had told him she'd be home late, so there was no need to hurry. So he dawdled, kicking a ball for a group of kids playing soccer, admiring a new motorbike parked in the street next to his, and detouring to the corner store to buy the latest instalment of his favourite superhero comic, *Batman*. Reaching his apartment building a short time later, he keyed in the entry code that made the heavy front door click open and went through the little courtyard beyond, past the cubby-hole where the caretaker Señor Santíago kept a watch on everyone's comings and goings. But today Emilio could hear the TV blaring – Señor Santíago was busy watching his favourite telenovela, the soap opera *Amor Bravio*.

He had just had a shower and was setting out his homework on the table when the key rattled in the door. 'Mamá, did you—' The words died on his lips as he saw his cousin Juanita in her city police uniform, her face strained, her eyes red. She wasn't alone. Beside her was a tall man in the black uniform of the Policía Federal, the Federal Police of Mexico.

Chapter 2

'**I'm sorry, I'm so sorry,** Emilio,' Juanita began, her voice breaking a little. Her hazel eyes were bright with tears.

Emilio hardly heard her. His stomach was heaving, there was a roaring in his ears. The Federal policeman said, 'My name is Raúl Castro, and I am an officer of the PF here in Mexico City.' He showed his identification. 'I regret to inform you that I have bad news.'

Emilio could hardly breathe. 'Mamá,' he whispered, 'is it Mamá – is she, is she . . . ' He could not finish the sentence. Dread filled him as his mind flashed back to the images he'd seen on TV at Nina's place. His mother, lying dead somewhere in a pool of blood . . .

Juanita read his expression at once. 'No, no, Milo,' she cried, 'she's not dead. She's—'

The policeman cut in quietly, 'Señora Lopez has disappeared and all the signs point to a kidnapping.'

Emilio stared at him. '*What?*'

'I understand it must be a terrible shock. Please be

reassured. We will do everything we can to find your mother and bring her safely home.'

Emilio was not at all reassured. 'But what if – what if you *don't* find her?'

'They will,' said Juanita shakily. 'Tía Gloria will be home in no time at all. You'll see. Now, Emilio, I'll help you pack.'

'Pack?'

'This is why I asked Officer Torres to come along with me,' said Castro. 'You can't stay here. It isn't safe.'

'You're going to come and stay with us, Milo,' said Juanita, and hugged him. 'We're family. We'll look after you.'

'A negotiator will be appointed as soon as possible but Officer Torres will also liaise,' said the policeman.

Struggling to control the shake in his voice, Emilio turned to Juanita and said, 'I want to know exactly what happened.'

The policeman began, 'I don't think that is a very wise—'

'Please, sir,' broke in Juanita. 'I think my cousin needs to hear this.'

Emilio flashed her a grateful look and stammered, 'Yes. Yes I do. Please.'

'Very well,' Castro conceded. 'At three-twenty this afternoon, a car was found abandoned in the carpark of the Hotel Paradiso. The hotel carpark attendant became suspicious after hearing a sound coming from the area where the car was parked.'

'A sound?' whispered Emilio, his imagination conjuring up horrible things.

'The sound you hear when a car door is left open – the alarm. And that's what the attendant discovered. Not only had the car door been left open but the key was still in the ignition. This car was clearly identified as a company vehicle belonging to Lopez Travel, from the logo on the door. And this was found on the ground close by.' He drew out a clear plastic bag from his pocket and took from it a small metal object.

Emilio recognised it at once. It was the little enamel medal of Our Lady of Guadalupe, the patron saint of Mexico, that his mother always wore around her neck on a thin silver chain. Millions of Mexicans wore the same medal but Emilio knew this one because of the tiny splash of blue paint on the back, from when his mum had been painting a cupboard years ago. She'd never been able to scrub it off. 'It's my mother's,' he choked.

'It must have been pulled off when she struggled,' said the policeman. 'The chain's broken. Like the car, it'll be dusted for fingerprints, and we'll see if any of them are useful to us, once your mother's have been eliminated. Though it's likely the kidnappers made sure they didn't leave DNA traces.'

'But surely . . . ' said Emilio. 'Didn't the attendant see anything? Mamá must have screamed, struggled!'

'Not necessarily. Going by what we know from other incidents, she was probably injected with a powerful tranquilliser that acted almost instantly. We believe she was probably snatched pretty much as soon as she parked and got out, although the attendant didn't notice anything for a good half-hour.'

'How come it took him so long?'

'He says he'd been listening to the radio – it was only when he switched it off that he heard the sound from the alarm.'

'But – do you believe him?'

'We can only go by that for the moment,' said the policeman smoothly.

'But someone else in the carpark might have seen something? Another motorist?' cried Emilio.

Raúl Castro shook his head. 'So far no one has come forward.' A pause. 'Of course, they rarely do.'

Emilio exchanged a look with his cousin. He understood what the policeman meant. People were too scared to come forward in cases like this. Violent men took bloody revenge if they thought you'd informed on them. Better to see nothing, hear nothing, know nothing.

'There are cameras,' went on Castro, 'however, they only cover the exit and entrance.' Seeing Emilio's expression, he added, 'But we might well get something useful from them.'

Emilio swallowed. He knew the policeman was trying to be reassuring, but that somehow made it seem worse. And there were so many things he didn't understand! Running a nervous hand through his thick dark hair, he said, 'But Mamá – why was she there in the first place? She doesn't have any clients in that area.'

'Staff at Lopez Travel informed us that Señora Mendoza Lopez had been called out to meet urgently with an important business contact who was staying at the hotel. An American named Señor Sellers. But there was something odd about this call.'

Emilio knew that Señor Sellers was one of the Holiday South people. He said, 'What? Surely he wasn't a part of this?'

'No, no. The call was *not* made by Señor Sellers,' said Raúl Castro. 'The city police spoke to him and found he knew nothing of any so-called appointment. When this was confirmed, they turned the case over to us as a probable kidnapping. We traced the call to your mother and found it was made from one of those pay-as-you-go cellphones, mobile phones you can buy from any street vendor.'

'But why – why would anyone want to kidnap my mother?' cried Emilio. He looked at Juanita. 'Tell him. Tell him. We're not rich or famous or important. It makes no sense.'

'No,' she said, 'it doesn't. It's wicked and pointless and—'

'Wicked, yes,' said Castro. 'Pointless, no. There is most certainly a point to this.' He paused. 'I believe there was an article in the local press a couple of weeks ago about the recent deal between your mother's company and an American travel agency, the one run by Señor Sellers. That's probably what triggered their interest in your mother.'

'You mean – they might have got the idea from that that Mamá is some sort of *tycoon* or something?' Emilio was horrified.

'Yes,' said the policeman. 'They might think she's richer than she really is. Or that she is *going* to be rich. People who are already wealthy have ironclad protection

– armed bodyguards and so on – and are much harder to kidnap. The gang that took your mother was looking for a softer target.'

Emilio felt sick. 'Do you know who . . . ?'

'No. Not yet.'

'But do you have any idea – any idea at all?'

'There are always ideas. Nothing firm, though. They'll be local if the article is what tipped them off.'

'That stupid article!' Emilio cried wildly. 'If only . . . '

He never finished his sentence, for just then the telephone on the wall began to ring.

Chapter 3

Emilio sprang for the phone, but Castro held up a hand. 'Wait. You have another phone here?'

'In the kitchen.'

'Good. I'll be listening. I'll give you a signal. When you pick up, just say your name. Don't say "Who's this?" or make any pleas or anything else. Understand?'

Emilio nodded, all his attention on the shrilling phone.

'Pick up on the count of three. One, two, three,' boomed Castro's voice from the kitchen.

Emilio snatched up the receiver. 'Emilio Mendoza Lopez here,' he stammered.

'Hello, Emilio.' It was the caretaker, Señor Santiago, and he sounded a little surprised by Emilio's shaky voice. 'A courier's just brought something for you. A large envelope, addressed to the Lopez and Torres families, marked Urgent and Important. Is your mother there?'

Señor Santiago must not have seen Juanita and Castro, Emilio thought. Juanita had a key to the apartment, so she wouldn't have needed him to buzz her through.

Emilio gabbled, 'No. She's not home yet. I'll – I'll come down right away.'

Raúl Castro appeared in the kitchen doorway with the phone to his ear, and shook his head meaningfully.

Emilio said, 'Actually, do you mind coming up with it?'

'No problem. But Emilio – is anything wrong?'

The policeman shook his head.

'No. No. Nothing's wrong,' lied Emilio.

'I'll be there in a few seconds, then.'

Emilio put the phone down. He looked at the adults. 'What should I do when he . . . '

'Put these on.' Raúl Castro handed Emilio a sachet containing a pair of transparent plastic gloves. 'Ask him to give you the envelope, and tell him to come in. But don't say anything to him about what's happened. I will need to speak to him. He may have some important information and it's best if he doesn't have time to think about it.'

It was at most a few minutes till the knock came on the door, but to Emilio it felt like hours of agonising waiting. When the rapping came he caught the Federal agent's warning glance and tried to master himself, but couldn't help fumbling as he opened the door.

'Ah, there you are.' The old man looked curiously at Emilio. 'So, what's up, eh?'

'No – nothing.' He held out his hand for the envelope.

'Have you been washing the dishes, Emilio?' Señor Santiago said, glancing at Emilio's gloved hands as he handed over the envelope. He laughed. 'What a pleasant surprise for your mamá.'

'No – er, yes,' said Emilio. 'Won't you – won't you please come in?'

'No, I—' Señor Santiago caught sight of Juanita and Castro, and his eyes bulged. He stammered, 'What – what has happened?'

'Please come and sit down, Señor,' said Castro. 'We just need to ask you some questions.'

'Questions?' repeated the old man, allowing himself to be led to a seat. 'Who are you? What's this about?'

The policeman identified himself and went on, 'I want to ask you some questions, Señor. 'He gestured for Emilio to hand him the envelope, having pulled on a pair of gloves himself. 'Can you describe to me who brought you this?'

The old man shot a look at Emilio, at Juanita. 'He – he was just ordinary.'

'How, ordinary? Young, old, middle-aged? Tall, small, fat, thin? Dark, fair, dressed well or badly?'

'I . . . I – well, he was young. Early twenties, maybe younger. Thin. Dark eyes. Dark hair, cut short, one of those razor-cuts.'

'Any distinguishing features?'

'Distinguish – oh, no. His face – it was just ordinary.'

'What sort of accent did he have?'

'He didn't speak. Just handed me the envelope and left.'

'His hands were bare?' There was hope in the policeman's voice.

'No. He wore gloves – you know, the kinds of gloves motorbike riders wear. I assumed he was one of those motorcycle couriers. They've come here before to deliver things.'

'But you hadn't seen this one before?'

'No, but then they change staff so often, those people.' He looked anxiously at Juanita, at Emilio. 'But what is this about? And where – where is Señora Lopez?'

Before either of them could answer, the policeman said, 'One moment. His clothes. What was he wearing?'

'Jeans. A jacket.'

'Colour, type?'

'Blue jeans. Black leather jacket. The rest – I don't know.'

'No logos or brands or symbols?' the policeman said.

Señor Santiago shook his head. He said, 'Nothing. Not that I saw, anyway.'

'We'll need you to come to the station, to help the police artist draw up an identity sketch.'

'An identity sketch!' The caretaker's eyes widened. 'What's happened?'

'Señora Lopez has disappeared. We believe she's been kidnapped.'

Shock flooded the old man's face. 'Madre de Dios! Kidnapped!'

All this while, Emilio had been half-listening to the interview, half-looking at the envelope in the policeman's hands. He longed for Castro to open it. Yet he wished he wouldn't. He needed to know what was in it, and yet he was terrified of what it might contain. Now, as the policeman slit open the envelope, his heart beat so fast and so loudly he was sure everyone could hear. He felt Juanita's hand on his shoulder tremble. Somehow that made him feel a little better.

With three pairs of eyes fixed on him, the policeman carefully pulled a single sheet of paper from the envelope. On it was a single printed paragraph. He read it out, slowly, each word piercing Emilio's mind like a red-hot needle

We have Señora Gloria Mendoza Lopez. She is safe and in good health and will remain so as long as our instructions are followed exactly. First, open an email account with this address and password ... Here Raúl Castro broke off. He looked at Emilio. 'I will brief Officer Torres later on the rest, and have this examined as evidence,' he said. 'For the moment, it is enough to know your mother is unharmed. He turned to the caretaker. 'Señor, we would appreciate it if you would say you know nothing if any neighbours start asking questions. Nothing at all, do you understand?'

Señor Santiago nodded and crossed himself, murmuring, 'And may the Virgin grant she stays safe,' and he put a hand on Emilio's shoulder. 'I am so sorry, Emilio, so very sorry.'

A wave of mixed relief and fear washed over Emilio. His mother was unharmed – but how long would she continue to be? Why had these people taken her?

Chapter 4

All the way to Tía Isabel's in the police car, Emilio sat silent. Earlier, he'd been able to ask questions. Now the shock had really set in. His brain felt frozen, his body disconnected. When the police car pulled up outside the Torres family's apartment block, he got out obediently, and waited while Juanita hauled his bag from the boot, then followed her and Castro into the building.

'Oh my poor Milo!' Tía Isabel exclaimed when she saw him. She wrapped him in a big hug. Her hazel eyes, so like her elder daughter's, were puffy and rather red, but she tried to smile as she led him into the apartment. 'You'll be safe here. Vicente's on his way from work, he'll be here soon. Luz!' she called out to her youngest daughter, Emilio's other cousin, who was hovering in the background. 'Take Emilio's bag.'

'You'll be in the spare room,' Luz gabbled, leading him down the passage, 'we've just made the bed. Mamá will make something to drink and . . . '

'Please, Tía,' Emilio whispered, 'do you think I

16

could – I could just sit in the bedroom a moment, by myself? I just need . . . '

'Of course,' said his aunt, kissing his cheek. 'Come on then, Luz, let's give Emilio some peace. And when you're ready . . . '

'Yes. I'll come out. Thank you,' said Emilio. When they'd left, he sat on the bed, hugging one of the bright cushions, trying desperately to hold on to some semblance of calm. He must stay strong. If he didn't, then he'd be no use to his mother. And he was determined to be, somehow. He didn't know how. Not yet.

How long he sat there, he wasn't sure, but by the time he roused himself and went back to the living room, Raúl Castro had gone, and Juanita was talking in a low voice to her mother and sister. They looked up when he came in.

'Are you feeling better, ciclito?' his aunt said.

He nodded.

'Good. You must not worry too much.' Her words were reassuring, but her red-rimmed eyes told a different story. 'It's all in good hands. Juanita says that policeman has much experience in these matters.'

Much experience in these matters . . . A little tremor went through Emilio. A terrifying world had come crashing into his own, and if he thought about it too much he would be overwhelmed. So he must not think about it. He must keep a clear head.

Luz patted the sofa next to her. 'Come and sit down, Milo,' she whispered. This wasn't the everyday Luz, with her messy hair and loud voice, but a big-eyed, alarmingly quiet and gentle version of her.

He sat down and, trying to keep his voice steady, said, 'What – what happens next, Juanita?'

'The email account mentioned in that note – that has to be created, with the username and password provided,' explained Juanita. 'Señor Castro said that's where the messages from the kidnappers will be left. Of course, as they made up the username and password, they can access it easily. But because it's not the kidnappers who have physically created the account, they can't be traced.'

'But when they send messages,' said Luz, frowning, 'won't they have to send it from a different account that *can* be traced?'

'No,' said Juanita. 'The note said that messages will be created in the account itself and left in the draft box instead of the inbox. And that means we have to use the same method – we can't send an email from that account to another but will have to reply using the draft box too. It's clever – and pretty much untraceable. But there'll be other avenues of investigation. You'll see. And the negotiator will help us.'

'The negotiator? Who's that?' asked Emilio.

'Someone experienced in these matters, lent by the Federales to help us,' said Juanita.

Emilio said, 'But the note was addressed to us, and sent to our apartment. Those people – they must expect *us* to answer, not someone else.'

Juanita nodded. 'They do. And that's why it must look as though it comes from us. But the negotiator will advise us on what to say and do. In theory, the Federal Police can't be officially involved in ransom negotiations. In practice, someone usually helps to advise the families privately.'

'Oh. So will it be Señor Castro?'

'No. He's an investigator, not a negotiator. We don't know who it will be yet. But we're to meet them tomorrow morning. If there's any communication from the kidnappers before then, we'll be informed immediately, of course.'

At that moment, the front door banged open, and an instant later Tío Vicente walked into the room.

Emilio's uncle was a large, jovial man with a booming voice and normally a big smile. Not today. He looked grey, his face drawn. Hurrying into the room, he hugged Emilio and shook his hand, up and down. 'So sorry, hombre. So sorry.'

Emilio gulped and nodded, not trusting himself to speak. Tío Vicente growled, 'We'll get those pendejos, you'll see, Milo.'

'Chente!' said Tía Isabel, automatically reproving him for swearing. But no one took any notice, least of all Emilio. Inside him, suddenly, fear was morphing into anger, into a wild fury. He imagined the pendejos, those rotten bastard kidnappers, on the ground in front of him, helpless, begging for mercy, and himself kicking them, over and over again till they stopped moving. They were faceless to him, inhuman, scum of the earth. He clenched his fists. 'I wish I was an adult. I wouldn't go by their rules. I wouldn't do as they said. I'd hunt them down, I'd kill them for what they've . . . ' But the words choked him, he couldn't bring any more out past the lump in his throat, and instead he just howled, the sounds tearing out of him.

Chapter 5

Emilio hardly touched his dinner, even though it was Tía Isabel's legendary albondigas, meatballs, and tres leches cake – a super-delicious cake which normally he'd have gobbled down in no time. After dinner, the whole family joined in a rosary of prayers, begging the Virgin and all the saints to protect Emilio's mother and bring her home safe. Emilio felt a little calmer, and back in his room, he clutched his mother's medal to him and whispered more prayers for her safety. Afterwards he fell into a restless, dream-haunted sleep.

In the morning, he woke to find it was already nine o'clock. Jumping out of bed, he checked his phone. He had messages. Just not from his mother, the one person he really wanted to hear from.

Meet tomorrow? read Sergio's text, while Pablo had sent him a picture message, showing the beach and Beatriz in the distance, in a white bikini. *Jealous yet?* was the caption. From his mother, silence. Emilio sent a quick text to Sergio, *Can't, sorry,* and another, *Enjoy,* to

Pablo, because if he didn't answer they might call him, and he didn't feel like talking to them. He'd have to tell them, but he couldn't. Not yet.

It was Saturday, but nobody else in the family had slept in. They were all up already, waiting for news. Waiting for the negotiator to show up with Castro, who'd called just a short while before.

This is the new normal, Emilio thought as he swallowed his breakfast eggs, cake and hot chocolate. A special breakfast. Everyone being super-nice to each other. It had a sinister holiday feel to it, a sense that real life had stopped, or at least paused.

'I called your grandfather in Mérida,' Tía Isabel said gently. 'I thought he should know. He is family. Despite everything.'

Emilio nodded. His father's father, Juán Garcia Lopez, and his mother had never seen eye to eye, and after Emilio's father Jorge died their relationship had become even more distant.

'He offered to help with money, but he also wanted to know if you would like to go and stay there for a while. It's a lot safer down there in the south-east, he says. And he's probably right.'

'No,' said Emilio sharply. 'I'm staying here in Mexico City. I want to. I have to! To do anything else – it would feel like running away!'

'That's what I said to him. He understood. He said he'd call you soon, and that he was thinking of you.'

There was a lump in Emilio's throat. He remembered

his grandfather and his mother having a terrible fight about where Jorge was to be buried: in the family plot in Mérida, or in Mexico City. Juán Lopez had won, and since then he and Emilio's mother had barely spoken. Emilio got on well with his grandfather and went to stay with him sometimes. He wasn't the hard, cold man Gloria thought he was. He was just proud, and found it hard to express his softer feelings.

'There's a taxi pulling up just outside.' Luz was at the living-room window, looking down into the street. 'Maybe it's them. Oh.'

'What's up?' said Emilio, knocking over his cup in his rush to get to the window too.

Two people were getting out of a taxi down in the street. Castro, in plain clothes this time, and another person, also in plain clothes: a young woman of about Juanita's age, dressed casually in a flowery top, jeans and sandals.

'She hardly looks old enough to be in the police, let alone be a negotiator with important duties,' grumbled Tío Vicente behind them.

'Hush, Chente,' said Tía Isabel sharply. 'You're not helping, with that kind of talk.'

'What kind of talk helps anyway, woman?' growled her husband. 'This is a very serious situation and they're about to inflict a little girl on us to advise us how to negotiate with dangerous criminals. Why not have just left it all to our daughter, if that was the case?'

'Oh, thanks very much, Papá,' said Juanita sarcastically. 'Glad you think so highly of my skills.'

'Stop it, both of you!' said Tía Isabel. 'Now's not the time to quarrel, when—' She halted as the entry phone buzzed.

Emilio's heart started pounding. *It's like yesterday,* he thought wildly. *Except now I know. Now I know it's not Mamá there. It's not going to be Mamá for a long . . . Shut up,* he told himself fiercely, *shut up. Yesterday you went to pieces. Today you are not going to. Do you understand, you tonto, fool? You have to stand tall. To be strong. You have to be a man, not a frightened little boy.*

He caught Luz's eye. She mouthed, 'You scared?'

He shook his head fiercely.

'I am,' she said quietly, and just then the knock came at the door.

Next to Raúl Castro, the young woman looked tiny, and her button-black eyes and black, dead-straight hair cut in a fringe gave her a rather doll-like appearance. But the gaze from those bright eyes was steely, her handshake firm and her voice sharp as a blade as she said, 'Good morning. My name is Alda Jiménez, and I am the appointed negotiator.'

Her calm manner steadied everyone right from the beginning, and as Castro described how she'd been involved in several successful cases, they began to feel better. He explained, 'As agents of the Federal Police, we are forbidden to enter into any ransom negotiations – I can only investigate the kidnap itself. Alda cannot officially deal directly with the kidnappers either – we keep our negotiators' identities secret for their own protection. But she will provide advice, coaching and support to you at every step of the way.'

'It's best if nobody knows I have anything to do with the police,' explained Alda. 'And as I will need to visit you frequently – perhaps even stay with you – till this situation is resolved, we must come up with a suitable story to explain my presence here to any curious neighbours.'

Juanita said, 'Mamá, how about if she poses as one of our Nicaraguan cousins, come to visit? Everyone knows you have relatives there but no one has met them.'

'Yes, it's a good idea,' said her mother. 'But how would you feel about it?' she asked Alda. 'You'd need to stay here.'

'All the better, as long as it suits you,' the young woman replied. Her serious face broke into a darting smile. 'I can easily do a Nicaraguan accent. I have a good friend who comes from there.'

'Then that's settled. Excellent,' said Castro. 'Now, let's get to work. Officer Torres, start up your computer. Go ahead, Alda, tell them where we're at.'

As Juanita booted up her laptop, Alda came straight to the point. 'This morning, the kidnappers sent their first message, with their demand. More importantly, they provided proof of life.' She saw their expressions and explained, 'It's always the first stage. There is no point in proceeding otherwise.'

Emilio trembled at these words. Luz moved closer to him.

Alda brought up a photo on her screen. 'It was sent as an attachment to the message in the draft box. I downloaded it here so you could see it immediately. As you'll notice, it was taken this morning.'

They all crowded around her to see. And there on the small screen was a photo of Emilio's mother, staring straight at them. She was dishevelled, had a bruise on one cheek and a small cut on her forehead, but the expression in her eyes was defiant. She was holding up the front page of a newspaper with the day's date on it.

'Those bastardos have hurt her,' growled Tío Vicente, clenching his fists.

'But look at her. She's so brave! She is not about to give up,' cried Juanita.

Luz looked at Emilio. 'Isn't she amazing?' she said quietly.

Emilio couldn't answer. What he was feeling was too big for words. It was made up of overwhelming relief and love, but also hate – burning hate for the cowardly, faceless creatures who for their own twisted reasons had hurt her, had forced his brave mother to do their will. He couldn't stop looking at his mother's face, but couldn't trust himself to speak.

'So,' said Tío Vicente. 'She's alive. And that's wonderful. But now tell us, why have the scum taken her? What do they want?'

The negotiator gave him a cool look. 'What they want is a great deal of money. Nine million pesos, or seven hundred thousand American dollars.'

Everyone gasped.

Tío Vicente barked, 'Nine million pesos! Absolutely ridiculous! Impossible. That's way beyond what we could even dream of raising! We're just ordinary people. Who do they think we are, Carlos Slim or someone?'

'Setting such a high price is an ambition only,' said Alda, unruffled. 'The starting bid, designed to make you feel grateful when they drop the price. As they will.'

'But how much – how much do you think they're prepared to . . . ' said Tía Isabel.

'In my experience, it drops steeply over time to something a family can afford.'

Over time – Emilio had once read about someone's kidnap ordeal. It had taken weeks and weeks for the police to find them, and by that time the victim, who'd been kept in a tiny dark room, was practically insane. Panic fluttered in his throat. He blurted out, 'Please – just how much time *do* we have?'

She gave him a cool look. 'It depends on who's got her.'

Raúl Castro cut in, 'We don't know who we're dealing with yet – or whether the motive is political, opportunist or personal, but—'

'Personal?' interrupted Tía Isabel sharply.

'Perhaps the mastermind is somebody known to Señora Lopez,' said the policeman. 'Somebody who bears her a grudge.'

'But that's ridiculous. My sister has no enemies!' snapped Tía Isabel.

'A disgruntled former employee, for instance,' said Castro, ignoring her.

'But – everyone likes my mother,' choked Emilio. 'She gets on really well with her staff. She's never sacked anyone. Never!'

Luz supported him. 'It's true. Tía Gloria is a good person. No one would ever hate her,' she cried, as the others nodded in agreement.

Castro said, 'We do consider it unlikely, because this crime was certainly carried out by professionals, not amateurs. Everything's been well planned and properly executed, with nothing left to chance, and their information was good. And the fact that there's been no other demand than money seems to argue against a political motive—'

'I should think so! Gloria doesn't have a political bone in her body,' interrupted Tía Isabel.

'Some radical group might have objected to her joining forces with an American company for political reasons, for instance,' went on Castro. 'But that doesn't seem to be the case as far as we know right now. If it's not political, then there is more hope for a speedy resolution. Political demands complicate matters. The American connection is important, though – it's given the kidnappers the idea that Señora Lopez has access to large funds, in American dollars.'

'That's an idea,' said Tío Vicente. 'I mean,' he said hastily as he saw their startled expressions, 'that the Americans might agree to help pay the ransom, once it's more reasonable—'

'Vicente!' said Tía Isabel crossly, just as Alda put in, 'My advice is not to mention them at all.'

'But we will still need to talk to them eventually,' persisted Emilio's uncle, 'because it's all very well to talk round and round this question, but the fact is, even if it's as you say and the kidnappers will take less than they've asked for, there's one certainty: these people are serious about getting paid a lot of money to release her. We want Gloria back, safe and sound. Therefore it follows that everything that has to be done will be. And that includes contacting the Americans.'

'Agreed,' said Alda. 'But it can wait.'

Emilio blurted out, 'Excuse me, but you said they were . . . ' – he gulped – 'professionals. Do you mean a kidnap gang?' He'd heard of such gangs before. Their main business was kidnap for ransom, and they snatched thousands of people every year.

Castro nodded. 'That is a possibility. However, it could also be somebody whose normal business is mainly in another area of crime.' He exchanged a meaningful look with Alda Jiménez. In a flash of insight, Emilio thought, *He's talking about the cartels. Drug dealers, that's who they think is behind it.*

His skin felt clammy as he remembered that story on the news, the bag of severed heads that had been left in the street not many kilometres from where they were right now. The drug cartels were merciless. Hideously cruel. Capable of anything. If his mother was in such hands, then what were her chances? He whispered, 'But Mamá has nothing to do with . . . ' He swallowed. 'With those kinds of people. So why?'

'Money,' said Castro. 'Just money.'

'But – but they make money, don't they,' Tía Isabel said. 'Lots of it. With their vile poisons. Much more than we could ever dream of. So why do they need . . . '

Castro said, 'Probably these people have had their trade interrupted by army or police action. It's quite likely, in fact, that that the group we're dealing with is not one of the big cartels, but a smaller gang that for some reason can't run their usual drug business. When that happens, they will often turn to this kind of crime to finance themselves.'

'Then do you know of any gang that has recently experienced such – such disruption?' said Emilio's uncle.

'Yes, I do. But we have nothing definite yet to tie any of them to this.' Castro paused. 'Please be assured,' he went on, 'that we will let you know as soon as we have more information, but until we have some firm leads, some hard evidence, I'm afraid it's useless to speculate further about the identity of these criminals.' He got up. 'Now, I must go, but I leave you in Alda Jiménez' capable hands. She will explain the next stage in the negotiating process.'

Tío Vicente seemed to be about to argue but Juanita headed him off. 'Thank you, sir,' she said. 'And may I relay any further questions we may have on the progress of the investigation to you?'

'Certainly, Officer Torres,' he said. 'At any time of the day or night, I can be reached on the numbers I gave you. Don't speak to anyone else about it, not even your colleagues.'

Emilio knew what this meant. Nobody else was to be trusted.

Castro was almost at the door when he turned. 'And may God and the Virgin be with you all,' he said gently, and let himself out.

Chapter 6

'Hmm,' Tío Vicente growled as the door closed behind the policeman. 'I hope he's not just relying on divine intervention to—'

'Hold your tongue for once, Chente,' snapped his wife. 'Alda,' she went on, turning to the young woman, 'please tell us, what happens next?'

'I will log you into the account we are using,' the negotiator said, 'but first we must discuss what you should say in the first message to the kidnappers. This will be in answer both to the proof of life demand, but also their first demand.'

She looked at Emilio and Luz. 'If you young ones feel scared or unsure, you don't have to—'

'No,' said Emilio sharply. 'I want to be a part of this. She's my mother!'

'I want to help too,' put in Luz. She looked pleadingly at her parents.

'We are all in this,' said Tía Isabel firmly, with a look at her husband as though she expected him to disagree.

Instead he said, 'We're a family, Señorita Jiménez. A family stands together. Especially at a time like this.'

'Fine. Well, then, it's important that you as a family should feel comfortable with my advice. You may of course disagree with my suggested course of action. But can I also say that a professional negotiator's advice should be trusted and followed if at all possible.'

They all nodded, except Tío Vicente, who said, 'Trust isn't something you give out like sweets from a piñata. The fact is, we don't know anything much about you, other than that you work for the Federales.'

'Papá!' said Juanita warningly, but he went on, 'And forgive me for saying so, but you don't look old enough to have had much experience.'

What is it with Tío? Emilio thought. *He's acting as though he's the boss of the family, as though Mamá is his sole responsibility. But he's only her brother-in-law. And I'm her son!* He wanted to say something cutting but couldn't. You had to have respect for your elders, even when they acted foolishly. He saw Luz roll her eyes.

But Alda Jiménez did not seem at all fazed. She gave a tiny smile and said, 'I understand your doubts. But let me reassure you that despite my age, I do have a great deal of experience. I have acted as negotiator in many successfully resolved cases of kidnap. And there's another thing you should know about me. I come from Juárez.' She paused to allow them to digest this and then went on, 'Yes, I'm from the most violent place in the country. We were pretty poor, but my parents brought us up well, and so my brother and sister and I never lost our way. Others we knew weren't so lucky. My own cousin Joaquin fell in with a bad crowd. He loved the whole gang thing, the guns, the easy money, the bravado, and he hero-worshipped the gang's leader. When you live in an atmosphere like that, nothing is normal. Joaquin started off in a small way, with petty thieving, then stealing cars, and he graduated to armed robbery. Five years ago he got involved in a plot to kidnap my mother's employer. The man was just a shopkeeper, but those greedy fools thought he was hiding the true extent of his wealth and decided they'd make his family cough up. Anyway, it all went wrong. There was a shoot-out. In the crossfire, the shopkeeper was seriously injured, and Joaquin was killed. It broke my aunt's heart. And broke up our family, because for a while my mother was under suspicion of having helped the gang. She lost her job. The shame of it burned her. And the pain of having been betrayed by her own flesh and blood, by her sister's son. She never really got over it.' Alda paused again. 'Now perhaps you can understand why I do this.'

There was a short silence. Then Tía Isabel said gently, 'Thank you for telling us.' She added, 'How do you think we should speak to these people?'

'Your message should be personal,' said Alda, 'but not too personal. Firm, but not aggressive. Willing to negotiate, but not desperate to close any deal. You've got to make them feel there are real people involved in this, but not try to touch them emotionally, because they won't be receptive. It is no use at this stage to ask them to transmit any kind of personal message to Señora Lopez, as first you must build their trust.' She saw their expressions. 'I know. It sticks in the throat. But it must be done, if this is to be handled successfully. Now then, you need to see the original message.'

They all waited with bated breath as she drew the laptop towards her, rapidly brought up a webmail site, typed in a username and password, clicked Enter, and brought up the account.

Welcome to your webmail, said an ironically cheery message in the inbox. In the box labelled 'Drafts' was a single number, in brackets: (1). Emilio's heart pounded as Alda clicked on it and the message opened. It had nothing in the 'To' line or the 'Subject' line, and was very short.

For the release of Gloria Mendoza Lopez, we demand 9 million pesos. Proof of life is attached. She will remain unharmed if you do exactly as we say. Write a message of agreement and leave in the draft box. Further instructions will follow.

And that was it.

Chapter 7

'**It's important that you react** correctly to this first message,' said Alda. That does not mean you have to agree with the size of their demand. What I suggest is that you write something very simple but personal, saying you are thankful for proof of life, and although the reward they request is beyond your financial capacity, you—'

'Wait a minute,' snapped Emilo's uncle, 'they didn't request, and it's not a reward, it's an extortion demand! These people are blackmailing scum!'

Tía Isabel quelled him with a look. 'Juanita, get some paper and a pen. We'll write something together,' she said. 'Please go on, Alda.'

'You need to make sure they understand you cannot pay that amount but you are willing to negotiate,' went on Alda. 'You should finish with something simple like "We await your further communication."'

Emilio's aunt began scribbling rapidly. 'What about this to start with?' she said, and read it out loud: '*My name is Isabel Mendoza Torres. I am Gloria's sister and speak for the whole family.'* Emilio made a little movement of protest. 'I know she is your mother, Milo,' she said softly, 'but it's best if an adult's name is on this. Do you understand?'

Emilio's throat felt tight, but he managed to say, 'Yes, Tía, I do.' And he did, in a way. The kidnappers were unlikely to take any notice of a thirteen-year-old boy, let alone think he was speaking for the family. But how he wished he was older! How terrible it was to be unable to do anything to help, not even something as simple as putting his name to a message!

'You're a brave young man,' said his aunt, flashing him a little smile and reading on. *'We are glad to have received proof my sister is alive and well.* Right – what next?'

'Please understand that the size of the reward you request for her liberation is well beyond our capacity to pay,' said Juanita.

'Yes,' said Tía Isabel, writing it down, *'but we are keen to continue negotiations and to this end are prepared to draw up financial statements so you can see what is possible.'*

'We await your communication,' Juanita said.

'In the expectation Gloria will remain unharmed,' finished her mother. 'And then I sign it. What do you think, Alda? Will it do?'

Alda nodded. 'Yes. It strikes the right balance.'

'I have to say it makes my hair stand on end, that we have to be so polite to these disgusting people,' grumbled Tío Vicente.

'Unfortunately that's the case, Papá,' said Juanita.

Emilio caught Luz's eye. He could tell from her expression that she was feeling as irrelevant as him. 'We are all in this,' Tía Isabel had said. And so they were. But when it came to the crunch, it was pretty clear that all the decisions lay with the adults, and Emilio and Luz could only look on.

It took a few more minutes for the message to be finalised and put in the Draft box. When it was done, Alda talked to them some more, while they kept a nervous eye on the webmail account, hoping the kidnappers would respond quickly. When they still hadn't done so more than an hour later, Alda left, accompanied by Juanita, to fetch clothes and other necessaries for her stay. They'd be back by lunchtime, they said.

While Tía Isabel went off to calm her nerves with preparations for a massive lunch, and Tío Vicente went off to calm his nerves with a quick drink at the local cantina, the cousins sat in the living room, half-heartedly watching TV while keeping an anxious eye on the laptop, just in case anything changed.

'Why in God's name haven't they answered already?' said Emilio for the umpteenth time, and for the umpteenth time Luz replied, 'They haven't logged into the account yet, that's all.'

He hoped she was right. He was afraid there was

another reason – that they'd been angry with the family's response and had taken it out on his mother. He didn't want to imagine how, but his mind kept sending up horrible images.

'She'll be all right,' said Luz. 'You'll see. She's a fighter, your mamá. And she's smart. She won't give up.'

'Yes,' said Emilio. He knew Luz was trying her very best to be positive, and so he tried to match her. 'She's probably thinking up ways of escaping them right now.'

'Yes, I bet she is!' said Luz. 'Hey, you know what,' she went on, her eyes widening. 'I've just thought of something!'

'What?' said Emilio cautiously. 'I've just thought of something' usually meant Luz had had a more than unusually wild idea.

'That medal they found – Tía's medal – you know how they said it only had her fingerprints on it?'

'Yes. So?'

'What if it didn't just come off when they took her? What if she deliberately broke the chain and left it there herself?'

'What?' repeated Emilio, baffled. 'Why would she do that?'

'As a clue, of course!' said Luz impatiently, tossing back her curly hair.

Emilio snorted.

'You can snort all you like,' huffed Luz, 'but it might mean something.'

'Like what?' said Emilio, one eye on the webmail, still frustratingly unchanged.

'Well, I don't know. But we might be able to work it out, if we think hard.'

Emilio shrugged.

'Don't you even want to think about it for one minute?' cried Luz. 'Isn't it better than just staring at that stupid, stupid screen hoping something will come up and hoping that everything's going to be all right if we just sit tight and do nothing?' The last words ended on a gasp as she burst into tears.

'It's okay, Luz,' he said, in a voice he tried hard to steady. 'It's okay. Please don't cry. I'm sorry.'

'Don't be silly! What do you need to be sorry for?' said Luz, fiercely wiping her eyes. 'It's a stupid idea, I know that, but my brain feels like a rat on a wheel and I feel I'm going crazy and I just don't know what to do.'

'Neither do I,' said Emilio sadly.

She flung her arms around him, and hugged him tight. 'Oh, I know, I'm sorry, Milo, I'm so sorry, I wish I – oh how I wish . . . '

'I know,' he said, hugging her back. 'I know, Luzita.' They sat in silence for a moment longer, then he said, 'You know what?'

'No,' she said, with a watery little smile.

'You're right. We can't just sit here and wait. We could do some research.' He gestured at the laptop. 'On the internet. See if we can find out a bit about – about the things Señor Castro was talking about. I mean, about the gangs that could be involved.'

'Oh,' breathed Luz, looking a little more cheerful now. 'Do you think we could find out who—'

'No,' he said honestly, 'but it's better than nothing, right?'

'Right!' she agreed.

Chapter 8

Well, that was a mistake, Emilio reflected some time later. All they'd done was fill their minds with dreadful statistics. Across Mexico, kidnappings had more than doubled in the last ten years, and there were now thousands of reported cases every year, carried out by drug cartels, specialised kidnap gangs, and simple opportunists. And that didn't include either unreported cases, or 'express kidnappings' in which victims were forced at gunpoint to withdraw all their money at ATMs before being released. The recorded cases were all people who had been abducted and held, imprisoned, for days, weeks, months, even years. The worst thing was the terrible images, photos sent by kidnappers of helpless victims bound and gagged.

'Look,' breathed Luz, pointing with a shaky finger at one photo of a blindfolded young man with a note pinned to his rumpled T-shirt: *Please pay them, Papá, or they'll kill me. I don't want to die.* 'What do you think – what do you think happened to him?'

Emilio whispered, 'I don't know. We can only hope that . . . ' He couldn't finish his sentence, but he knew Luz knew what he meant. Kidnappers often treated victims badly, at the least locking them up in cramped and uncomfortable rooms, and sometimes beating, starving and torturing them. Worse, some gangs killed hostages even after they'd been paid a ransom. It seemed that most victims were released alive, but very few kidnappers were ever brought to justice. There were just too many cases for the police to investigate. Worse, kidnap gangs were sometimes protected by corrupt police, or even run by them.

No Mexican could ignore these things completely, but Emilio lived in a relatively safe part of Mexico City and for him and the people he knew, the underground war that raged in his country – the killings, the gun battles, the disappearances, the kidnappings – had always been a sinister rumble in the background. It wasn't like Juárez here. Oh, everyone everywhere knew to be careful. You knew that there were districts you should never go to under any circumstances, and some that might be safe during the day but not at night. You knew that you should never hail a taxi on the street but always call one from a trusted company, and that motorists didn't have to stop at red lights after 10 p.m. but were allowed to go straight through, because to stop meant you might be carjacked. These kinds of precautions were part of ordinary, everyday life because violence was an ever-present possibility, but despite all that, nothing of the kind had ever happened to anyone Emilio knew – until now. Now he was willy-nilly caught up in the conflict. What was reported in article after article was no longer something he could click out of and then turn away from with relief. Now, the rumble was a roar, the war had exploded into his family's midst, and normal life seemed suddenly as far away as the moon.

When you live in an atmosphere like that, nothing is normal. That's what Alda had said, speaking of her cousin Joaquin. And the stories he and Luz had just read made that very clear. In this terrible civil war, the old ways of Mexico were being destroyed. People who tried to take a stand were often threatened, beaten, even brutally murdered. Oh, there were many tales of heroism, too, like the one about Marisol Valles Garcia, the 20-year-old who'd become a police chief because she wanted to make a difference, or the teenage 'angels' who stood on street corners with placards pleading with gangsters to give up their evil ways. But all too often it ended badly – the young police chief had to flee to the US in fear of her life, and the 'angels', spooked by threats, vanished from the streets. And the carnage continued. Helpless illegal immigrants from Guatemala and El Salvador were forced to become drug mules and were then slaughtered and thrown into mass graves in the desert. Tens of thousands of children had been orphaned by the violence, and boys and girls as young as ten had turned into hardened criminals who killed without a shred of pity.

Suddenly Emilio could not bear to read even one more word. He closed down the window.

'Hey! I was reading that!' protested Luz.

'Well, that's too bad. I've had enough,' snapped Emilio. Nothing had changed on the webmail window, so he closed that down too and slammed the laptop shut. 'I need some air.'

'I'll come with you,' said Luz, jumping up.

'No you won't,' said Tía Isabel, coming into the room at that moment, wiping her hands on her apron. 'Neither of you will go anywhere till Alda's back, is that clear?'

Luz shot a glance at Emilio. She began, 'But, Mamá—'

'But nothing. You both stay here.' Tía Isabel looked at Emilio. 'There's no new message, is there, Milo?'

He shook his head.

'It'll come. You'll see. Juanita just texted to say they're on their way back. I've called Vicente too. Now come to the kitchen. I've just made agua fresca. And we can have something to nibble on till they all get back.' Her voice was full of a brittle cheerfulness that didn't fool Emilio for a second, but a couple of minutes later, seated in the cosy kitchen with a tall glass of the refreshing iced drink, made with watermelon, and a bowl of Tía Isabel's special chilli peanuts in front of him, he realised not only how thirsty and hungry he was, but how much he wanted *not* to think about what had happened, if only for a few minutes. Just for a little while, he wanted to pretend that he was just visiting his aunt and uncle for Saturday lunch and in the afternoon he'd meet up with his friends and they'd hang out, talk, play computer games, maybe listen to music—

His friends! They didn't know anything about what had happened. And he shrank from telling them. He didn't want to have to go through the 'Oh my God, this is so terrible, oh my God, what can we do—' conversations. It wouldn't help. Not at all.

Chapter 9

Later, as Luz and he were setting the table – still with no new message in the webmail account – he asked his aunt, 'Why hasn't there been anything about Mamá's kidnapping on the radio or the local newspaper?'

'Because the police don't think it's a good idea just yet, cielito,' she said, deftly patting tortillas into shape before cooking them on the stove. She'd made lots of food: caldo de res, a hearty beef and vegetable soup, juicy pumpkin and sweet potato empanadas, arroz con pollo, fragrant chicken with yellow rice, an array of colourful salads made with corn, tomatoes, avocados, peppers and black beans, and for dessert a flan con nata, a crème caramel with whipped cream. And to drink they had agua fresca of two kinds, the watermelon one and also mango. She was always a good cook and today, she'd been driven by the need to distract herself. Emilio couldn't help feeling his mouth water, despite the worry about this mother.

'Why don't they think it's a good idea, Tía?' he asked, sneaking an empanada.

'Because it's better if the kidnappers can't get any information. Maybe later, if the police think it will jog someone's memory, then we'll do something. For the moment, they're trying to keep it out of the news. Just as they've asked us to make sure none of us says anything on any social media. You haven't, have you, Milo?'

Emilio shook his head. The last thing he wanted to do was to share this horror on Facebook. But he wasn't sure what to think about the police view on publicity. Surely someone would eventually talk. Would it make things worse if they did? Did the kidnappers want their crime to be kept a secret, or to be known? You'd need to think like a criminal to know that.

Think like a criminal. It must be what Alda had to do, in her job, day after day after day, constantly trying to outwit ruthless people who lived by their own wicked wits.

He shivered. He really should not have looked at all those stories on the internet. Now he couldn't stop thinking about them.

The front door banged. Once, twice. Emilio could hear Tío Vicente's voice raised in boisterous chatter. He must have had a few Cervezas too many. Tía Isabel's lips tightened, but she said nothing.

'Wow,' said Juanita, as they all came in together, with Alda carrying an overnight bag. 'You *have* been cooking up a feast, Mamá!'

'That's my Chavelita,' said Tío Vicente, 'what a good woman,' and he tried to plant a sloppy kiss on his wife's

cheek. She stepped away briskly. 'Come, Vicente,' she said
warningly. 'We have a guest. Remember? Now sit down.'

'A guest? Oh, that's right,' said Emilio's uncle. 'Ah
yes, our cute little Nicaraguan cousin,' and he winked
at Alda.

She didn't look embarrassed. But Juanita was, and so
was Luz, while Tía Isabel looked furious. Emilio couldn't
help a tiny inward smile. His uncle's naughty behav-
iour was oddly comforting. He hardly touched drink
during the week, but at weekends he relaxed, meeting
local cronies at the cantina to drink beer and tequila,
play cards, gossip, listen to music. He was never a mean
drunk. Clownish, yes. Silly, certainly. Annoying, often.
But never mean, never shouty, never violent. After lunch
he'd probably fall fast asleep on the sofa in front of the
football or the boxing, and snore. He always did that on
a Saturday afternoon.

'Please help yourself,' said Tía Isabel to Alda, deliberately ignoring her husband.

'Thank you. It looks muy delicioso.' Alda had her
phone out on the table next to her and as the dishes
were passed around, Emilio noticed that she glanced at
it more than once. (The laptop, though, had been left
on the living-room table.) Staring at the screen was like
willing a maths lesson to end, he thought. It wouldn't,
if you watched the clock. You had to not look, pretend
you didn't care. Only then would the time slip by, as if
it thought it had tricked you.

'Do you like music, Señorita?' Tío Vicente gazed
earnestly at Alda.

49

'Please, call me Alda,' said the investigator.

'Alda, then. What sort?' he persisted.

'Guitar, ballads, that kind of thing.'

He beamed. 'You have good taste! My friend Miguel, he brought his guitar to the cantina today, and we sang the old numbers. You'd have enjoyed it, Alda – real music, not like that silly rubbish Milo likes, what is it, that one where they don't even sing properly, they just talk and say swearwords all the time?'

'Rap, Tío,' said Emilio. 'It's called rap.'

'Yeah. That. What has this gringo music got to do with us Mexicans? As if we don't have to put up with enough from north of the border, must they corrupt even our musicians with that tuneless nonsense?'

'But Tío,' hazarded Emilio, 'there are many Mexican rap artists and—'

'Ay, no! They're not real Mexicans, those ones.'

Emilio shrugged, and exchanged a wry glance with his cousins.

'Chente, I'm sure Alda does not want to listen to your theories,' cut in Tía Isabel sharply. 'And I for one hope you kept your mouth shut in front of your amigos in that cantina, songs or no songs.'

'What are you saying, woman? That I cannot be trusted to keep a secret? Do you think I have lived all the years of my life without knowing how to keep my mouth shut?' His voice rose. 'But is there any reason for it to be kept shut now, at my very own table in my very own house?'

'Papá,' said Juanita pleadingly.

He glanced at her, and the anger in his eyes vanished, to be replaced by a sheepish look. 'I'm sorry,' he muttered. 'This business – it's made me jumpy. Made me forget my manners. Forgive me, everyone. You especially, Milo,' he went on, patting his nephew's hand.

'It's all right, Tío,' said Emilio, even more awkwardly. 'Don't worry about it.'

'Ah, you're a good boy. Gloria brought up a good boy, didn't she, Chavela?' said his uncle fondly.

'Yes. She did,' said his aunt quietly, the impatience wiped from her face. 'And I know she is very proud of him.'

I wish they wouldn't talk about me as though I'm not here, thought Emilio. *And I wish they wouldn't praise me like that. It makes me feel even more that things aren't normal, that they think there's no hope, no clue to go on.* His eyes prickled, and to stop himself from crying he made himself stare at a bracelet Alda had on, made up of different little cameo images of Our Lady of Guadalupe, with her sweet face and her starry blue veil and her—

'Oh my God,' he said, jumping up from his place so suddenly that he knocked over his chair with a crash. 'I've got it, I've got it!'

Five startled faces turned to him. He hurried on, 'I mean, it was Luzita's idea really, and I didn't think much of it then, but what if it was right, if it wasn't them who ripped it off but Mamá who pulled it off herself when they didn't notice?'

'What *are* you talking about, Milo?' said his aunt.

'The medal,' said Juanita sharply, 'that's what you mean, isn't it?'

'Yes,' said Emilio. 'Luz thought that Mamá might have meant it as a clue, and—'

'It was just an idea,' began Luz, 'because of the fingerprints . . . '

Alda held up a hand to quieten her. 'Go on, Emilio,' she said.

'Well, I remembered that Señor Castro had said the kidnappers possibly wore gloves and also cover-up clothes – long sleeves, hats, things like that, and I wondered how no one had noticed someone dressed like that, and then I was thinking of what Luz said, and I saw Alda's bracelet, and I thought – well, what if the clue was about that?'

'I mean,' he hastened on as he saw their utterly baffled expressions, 'what if they were covered up in a way that you wouldn't notice, because it would look completely normal? But that might remind you of the picture on the medal?'

Everyone stared at him. Tío Vicente said, his voice quite sober now, 'You surely don't mean that whoever took your mother was dressed like Our Lady? Everyone would notice if—'

'No,' said Alda. Her eyes were very bright. 'No, that's not what he means. Is it, Emilio? You mean your mother was desperately trying to leave something behind, something that might give us at least a little to go on. The kidnappers weren't dressed *exactly* like Our Lady. That is, not in the same colours. But they wore veils. And long robes.'

'Nuns!' Juanita exclaimed, staring at Emilio. 'You think Tía Gloria might have been trying to tell us *the kidnappers were dressed as nuns.*'

'Excuse me,' said Alda, 'I must make a call at once.' And she picked up her phone and dialled, putting it on speakerphone so they could all hear. 'Raúl? Something's come up.' Rapidly, she told him Emilio's idea.

When she'd finished, Castro said, 'We'll check with the attendant right away if he saw any nuns yesterday. Check other witness statements, too. And the vehicle exit and entrance footage, just in case we can spot a car with nuns in it.' He paused, then said, 'Emilio?'

'Yes, Señor?' said Emilio, a little unsteadily.

'It's a clever idea. But don't pin your hopes on it, will you? Just in case.'

'No, Señor.'

'When will you – when might you know if it's a possibility?' said Tía Isabel.

'I can't give you a definite time on that. But I'll be as quick as I can.' He hung up.

Tía Isabel turned to Alda. 'Now let's go and check that wretched laptop again.'

They did, and there was still nothing. But the stubbornly unchanged screen didn't make Emilio feel quite as helpless as it had before. At least in a small way he and Luz had contributed to the hunt for his mother. For the first time in two days, he was almost pleased with himself. And that felt good.

Chapter 10

Raúl Castro called back a couple of hours later. 'We might be onto something. I went back to the attendant and asked him if he'd seen any nuns in the carpark at any stage. He said that he did remember some, driving out in a van some time that day. He only remembered because the three of them were all sitting in the front. He didn't remember much about their appearance – of course you don't tend to look too much at nuns, they're not like other women. But he thought one of them was small, while the others were larger. They all wore full habits and veils, and sunglasses. And that's it.'

'Were they actually women?' said Alda.

'With that sort of description and in those sorts of clothes, they could be either. They didn't have moustaches or beards, anyway. He'd have certainly remembered that! But he only vaguely recalled their van – couldn't tell us the make, only that it was light-coloured, dusty and not new. We're checking the carpark footage right now for it. Wait a moment – they've found something.'

Everyone held their breath. Emilio's heart pounded. *Don't pin your hopes on this*, he told himself. *Don't. Don't.* But he couldn't help the excitement rushing through his veins. He met Luz's glance. She crossed her fingers.

'We have an old-style, beige-coloured Ford van answering that general description, exiting the carpark about twenty minutes before the attendant found the car,' said Castro, coming back on line. 'Unfortunately we can't see the driver or passenger's faces, because the windows are tinted. We can see the driver's arm as they lean out to pay the attendant, and the back of a veiled head, so it looks as though there were nuns in it or at least someone dressed as a nun. But the number-plate's half-obscured by dust. We'll enhance both images and see what we can come up with by morning. We're checking now for when the van entered the carpark and how that fits in with when Señora Lopez came in. My instinct is that they would already have been there when she arrived, and that they snatched her as soon as she opened the car door. We'll be able to put an exact timing on that very soon.' He paused. 'However, I must stress to you that even once we know the numberplate, it is a strong possibility that we will find out that these were perfectly innocent nuns who had nothing whatever to do with what happened. And so my original advice still stands: don't pin your hopes on this.'

'Easier said than done,' said Tío Vicente gruffly, as the call ended.

Exactly, thought Emilio. How could you not hope this was the lead they needed?

'Besides,' said Juanita thoughtfully, 'it's got to be them. Or what were three nuns doing in the carpark of the Paradiso hotel?'

'You're right. It's a smart hang-out,' said Tía Isabel, 'not a charitable foundation. What business would they have there, if they were innocent?'

Alda smiled. 'They could be canvassing for donations.'

'Ha! Maybe they were. The wrong sort,' said Tío Vicente grimly.

As the hours dragged on towards late afternoon, Emilio felt the strong hope that had filled him earlier begin to fray. No more news from Castro. Nothing in the webmail. Everyone tried to keep their spirits up but there was just so much you could repeat about the three nuns and the medal and the possibility it might all lead somewhere. After a while he couldn't bear to sit in the living room any more listening to the adults going over and over the questions. But he didn't want to be on his own either, so instead of going to his room he went along with Luz to hers. They didn't chat much at all. Luz lay on her bed and read a book, while Emilio sprawled on her rug with a cushion and his iPod. Instead of enjoying his usual playlist he found himself searching for songs his mother might like – bright mariachi band music, party music, dance music. She was such a sensible person mostly, brisk, organised, efficient, but she had another side to her too, a side that loved to let go. She wasn't a particularly good dancer, just a very enthusiastic one. Emilio had found it embarrassing at times, but now he'd give anything to have her dancing wherever and however she wanted, as loud, clumsy and embarrassing as she wanted to be, and he'd cheer her on!

Mistake. The tears were welling up in his eyes again. Hastily, he switched off the iPod. He said, 'Luz, do you have something I could read? Something totally—'

He never finished his sentence because at that moment Juanita came in without knocking. Her face was pale. 'You'd better come. There's another message.'

'What is it? What does it say?' Luz cried, struck by her sister's grim expression. But Emilio could not speak. Fearing the very worst, he pushed past them both and ran into the living room. His aunt and uncle were sitting at the laptop. Tía Isabel was weeping. Tío Vicente was trying to comfort her. Alda was on the phone in the corner of the room, talking softly, urgently.

His aunt looked up and saw him. 'Oh, cielito . . . Your mother – she has written a letter – it's . . . '

The relief of it was so big it felt like a punch to the chest. If she was writing letters then she couldn't be d– But he couldn't bring himself to finish the word, even in his thoughts. He said, 'Please. I have to see.'

They turned the screen towards him, and there was a PDF, a scan of a handwritten letter. It was his mother's writing, definitely. He read it quickly.

Please dear sister please dear family do as they say or they will kill me. Use all my money. My accountant will give you all details. Use everything you can. Ask anyone you can.

And you must speak to the Americans. Move quickly. Money is nothing. Life is everything. Think of me. Think of my little heart, my own Emilio.

It was signed *Gloria*.

Yes, it was her writing. But the words – they weren't like her, nor was that pleading tone, that willingness to give in. And those words 'corazoncito mio' – 'my little heart' – she'd never called him that before. The kidnappers must have dictated the whole thing to her, stood over her to make her write it. Tears burned at the corners of Emilio's eyes but he refused to shed them, clenching his fists tightly instead.

Juanita said, 'It came as an attachment. To their message.' She clicked into the Drafts box. The message was short and aggressively questioning.

What is your sister's life worth to you, Isabel Mendoza Torres? What does her son's happiness mean? Why haven't you sought funds from everywhere? And why haven't you spoken to the Americans already? Do so, then we will contact you again.

'How dare they! Those thieves, those brutes, those sons of . . . ' exploded his uncle. 'If I had them here, I would grind their intestines for chorizo, I would mash their faces into pulp, I would—'

'Please,' said Emilio, breaking into his uncle's rant, 'please, Tío Vicente, please Tía Isabel, we must make the Americans see that they must help us, help my mother, we must—'

'Of course we will, Milo, of course we are,' said his aunt, putting an arm around him. 'Tonight, if we can.

Alda is making some calls to arrange it. And she says –
she says . . . ' Her voice wavered, then steadied. 'She says
that though it's frightening to read what they say, to read
your mother's . . . what it really means is that they are
getting ready to negotiate.'

'Or they wouldn't be asking those questions,' put in
Alda. 'They'd just say there's no bargaining at all. And,'
she went on, turning to Emilio, 'I know it was hard for
you to read your mother's letter. But think of this. These
people – that's what they thrive on. That's what they
count on. Other people's misery. They want Isabel to
feel guilty about not giving in, they want you all to panic
as a family, and they want you, Emilio, to think of your
mother as beaten down and cowed. But just because she
was compelled to write those words doesn't mean that
in her heart she has given up. Only a fool is outwardly
defiant with a gun against the head. And from everything
I hear about her, your mother is no fool.'

Their eyes met. He choked out, 'No. She's not.' With
those words Alda had made him feel better in a way that
no one in his family could have done. She'd seen and
heard these things many times before, and so her words
rang with truth. The truth of experience.

Chapter 11

Emilio slept badly that night. He kept waking up from horrible nightmares, hideous scenarios spooling out like deranged films, and he found it hard to go back to sleep.

The meeting with the Americans had been set for the following morning at ten o'clock, right after a meeting with the Lopez Travel accountant, who'd give them written confirmation of available funds. Emilio's aunt and uncle and Juanita were to meet Señor Sellers and his associate in a coffee shop only a few doors down from Lopez Travel. The location had been deliberately chosen as one the kidnappers were likely to be watching, so they'd know the meeting with the Americans that they'd demanded was going ahead. This would help to protect Emilio's mother, Alda had explained. Alda herself would not be going to the meeting – to do so would compromise her cover story as a mere distant cousin. She was staying in the Torres flat with Emilio and Luz.

But what if things went wrong, Emilio kept thinking as he tossed and turned. What if the Americans refused to help, or the kidnappers decided to snatch more members of the family? Alda had assured them that it wouldn't happen. There would be surveillance – discreet, of course – from Castro's men. They would be on the lookout for any suspicious activity – anyone who seemed to be taking too much interest or loitering too close to the coffee shop, for instance. But, Emilio thought, the kidnappers had planned their crime carefully, snatched his mother in broad daylight without being seen. They'd hardly be stupid enough to be caught 'loitering', would they?

He woke from a nightmare at half past five and couldn't go back to sleep, try as he might. So he gave up and tiptoeing past the living room, where Alda was fast asleep on the sofa, he went to the kitchen. He found Luz sitting by herself at the table, drinking a glass of pineapple juice.

'Hey. So you woke early too,' she said.

'Yes.'

Luz went on, 'Do you think it's going to work?'

'What?'

'The meeting. Do you think the Americans will agree to pay anything?'

Emilio shook his head. 'I have no idea.'

'Have you met that Señor Sellers? What's he like?'

'I met him just once, when I'd called round to Mamá's office. He seemed nice and he spoke fluent Spanish. His wife's Mexican, he told Mamá, she's from Hermosillo, so he knows our country well, they're often here. Mamá said he seemed like a good man. They got on well.'

'Then he would want to help her!'

'Maybe. But it's not just him, is it. That other guy, his business partner, Señor Taylor, who's also going to be at the meeting, he's not going to think the same way. He doesn't know Mamá personally – he was supposed to meet her at the party.' He swallowed. The party. He'd not looked forward to it, he'd thought it would be so boring, but now he would have given anything to have it. The party should have been on last night. The Lopez Travel staff had had to call everyone and tell them it was being postponed, citing his mother's 'illness' as a reason. That was before it had been decided that Señors Sellers and Taylor must be brought into the negotiations.

'Americans have plenty of money,' Luz said. 'And I've heard they can be very generous.'

'Maybe. But it's not really their problem, is it? It's not happening to their family. They'll probably feel sorry for us. But—'

'But you two are up far too early,' said Juanita, appearing at that moment. 'What's going on?'

'Couldn't sleep,' said Emilio and Luz, almost in unison.

'Can't say I did too well myself,' said Juanita, rattling around with coffee pot and cups.

'What do you think, Juanita?' asked Luz.

'About what? Oh, the Americans.' She glanced at Emilio. 'I think we have to wait to find out. But you must not focus too much on it. I hope that soon we will have more news about the van and the so-called nuns. Raúl Castro might be well on the way to catching these people.'

'Do you really think so?' said Emilio eagerly.

'I think it is very possible,' she said.

Very possible wasn't the same as *sure* or *definite*. All the same, it was something.

They still hadn't heard from Castro by the time Juanita and the others had to leave. Emilio and Luz watched them go from the window. He was trying not to feel nervous, trying to persuade himself that everything would be okay. Nobody would attack them. The Americans would say yes. All that he and Luz had to do was sit around and wait. But waiting was hard. So hard.

Juanita texted Alda soon after ten to say they'd just met up with Señors Sellers and Taylor. She'd let Luz and Emilio know when the meeting was over. But one hour, two hours, nearly three hours ticked by, and still there was no word. Emilio and Luz spent most of that time watching TV, while Alda sat with them, reading a book. And then, just after the text came from Juanita to say the meeting had finished, a call came in to Alda from Castro. The van's numberplate had been traced and its owner identified. Unfortunately, that didn't help in the search for the kidnappers.

'It was stolen the morning of the kidnapping,' he said on speakerphone. 'The owner didn't even know it had been taken till the late afternoon. We've issued an alert but it's likely they'll have ditched it by now.' Emilio's heart sank. 'But don't be too disappointed,' the policeman went on. 'This is an important development. Even if they destroy the vehicle, I'm fairly confident now it was the one used in the kidnap. We also know where the van was stolen, and neighbours are being questioned. It's possible someone might remember something.'

'And the driver, sir?' asked Alda. 'You said there was some progress made on that too.'

'A little. Enhancement did not reveal his face – unfortunately that remains obscured – but we came up with a detail on his forearm. Where the sleeve fell back as he paid the attendant, you can see part of what we believe may be a gang tattoo.'

'Which, sir?' breathed Emilio.

'We're not sure yet. The image needs further enhancing, so it's been sent out to a specialist laboratory. You will be informed as soon as we know more.' He rang off.

Emilio said, 'Is it really true, what he said? I mean about it being an important development? He wasn't just saying that to make us feel better?'

Alda smiled. 'I can't say he didn't want to do that. But it's true nevertheless.'

'This tattoo – will it prove what gang's involved?'

'I wouldn't go that far. But it may prove helpful.' She glanced out of the window. 'They're back. Good. I was beginning to be a little concerned.'

❖

Tío Vicente said that the meeting with the Americans had gone as well as could be expected, but had not yielded any firm promises yet.

'Señor Sellers – he said he understood completely and really wanted to do something,' said Tía Isabel. 'He feels responsible in a way, because of the article, though I told him it wasn't his fault.'

'But his friend is less keen,' broke in Tío Vicente, 'and said they'd have to see how it could be done without attracting the wrong sort of attention. No idea what he meant because we've already got the wrong sort of attention, but you know what Americans are like, they like to talk for nothing sometimes.'

'That's unfair, Papá,' said Juanita, 'you know it's a difficult situation for them too.'

'Not half as hard as it is for us,' said her unrepentant father. 'I didn't much appreciate Taylor asking us about Gloria's kidnap insurance – as if he doesn't know insurance companies will never help with a ransom! You have to claim afterwards, once you've lost all your money. And—'

'We're going to have to wait anyway,' said Tía Isabel, cutting him off, 'until our American friends tell us what they can do. They said they'd let us know as soon as possible. But we have to tell the kidnappers something now,' she added anxiously, turning to Alda.

'Yes, you do,' said Alda, 'but we'll make sure it's said in a way that doesn't pin it down too specifically. Don't worry, I'll help you with that.'

Chapter 12

We have Gloria's financial information, as well as
what we can raise ourselves from other family. It is attached
here. And we met the Americans. They request an interview
with Gloria, on the phone, in our presence, before they will
agree to anything. We beg you to allow this to happen as soon
as possible.

The message had been put in the Draft box, and
now there was only waiting. The Americans had not
actually asked to speak to Emilio's mother on the phone,
but had promptly agreed once the idea – suggested by
Alda – was put to them. It was all a gamble. A gamble to
get some small advantage. For according to Alda, if the
kidnappers agreed to let Emilio's mother speak, then it
was possible some information might be gleaned from
the call. Not a location – the kidnappers were certain
to use an untraceable 'burner' phone like the one they'd
used to lure Gloria to the carpark – but something else,
however small. A sound. A slip-up of some sort. Some
kind of clue.

And if they didn't agree? Alda said that was unlikely. 'They want the money,' she said. 'And besides, you've begged them, reinforcing the feeling that they have all the power. They may take some time to agree, but I think they will in the end. Because if they do so, they know you will be grateful. And that makes them feel even more powerful.'

It was utterly disgusting, thought Emilio. It made him feel sick and ashamed. Because they had to beg. Because they had to go by these vicious people's rules. Because neither the family nor the police could do anything for his mother except try to placate and second-guess ruthless criminals. There was nothing they could do to protect her.

That morning they all went to Mass, and afterwards lit candles for the safe return of Emilio's mother. The priest, Padre Alfonso Benitez, came over to talk to them while they were there – he knew the Torres family well – and he was so kind that it made tears come to Emilio's eyes. 'If I can be of any help,' he said, 'don't hesitate to call on me. Any time, day or night.'

They'd only just got back to the flat when a call came from Castro. He had two pieces of news to give them: the van had been found, but as expected, burned out on a back road out of the city. And the tattoo had been identified as an image of the so-called 'narco-saint', San Jesús Malverde. This information did little to lift Emilio's bleak mood. The fire that had destroyed the van had also destroyed any possible fingerprints or DNA evidence; and as to the tattoo, it was hardly an unusual one among criminals. About the only concrete thing it indicated was that the man could be from the north, specifically from Sinaloa Province where the cult of Malverde had originally been based.

Emilio knew that Malverde was an armed robber who was supposed to have committed crimes to help the poor against oppressive landowners in the early 1900s. After his hanging in 1909 some people started saying he was a saint, and though the Church tried to stamp out the idea, it grew and grew among the poor, but also among criminals. Now 'San Malverde' had become famous throughout the country as a patron saint of drug dealers. There were shops where you could buy busts and medals of 'the narco-saint', complete with smart white shirt and big black moustache, as well as souvenir Malverde T-shirts, soaps, glasses, mugs, a whole host of things: it was quite an industry, for there were hundreds of thousands of his devotees. Just about everyone who venerated him had some link to crime.

It was hardly the vital clue they'd been looking for, but Castro had said that it would still be followed up. 'We'll visit the places where Malverde devotees hang out in the city,' he said. 'Whether or not anyone can or wants to give any useful answers is another matter. If they're not involved, they'll be scared of those who are.'

'Don't be too discouraged,' added Alda, seeing Emilio's crestfallen expression. 'Someone might let something slip, without even knowing it. It is a break.'

'We've certainly got more information now,' agreed Castro. 'Information the kidnappers don't know we have.

And that's useful. The investigation is certainly moving.'

But at snail's pace, thought Emilio. How long could his mother last? How long before the kidnappers lost patience with stalling tactics?

The grown-ups decided it wasn't safe for Emilio to go to school.

'Once the weekend is over,' said Tía Isabel, 'we must tell your teachers what is going on and why you can't go to classes for the next while. It's time you told your friends too.'

'Yes, we agree it's better not to let rumours take hold,' said Alda. 'But remember to give them just the bare facts, no detail. Don't mention me at all, and don't tell even your best friend where you are.'

That evening he called his friends and finally broke the news to them. It was hard, listening to them struggling to express what they felt. Sergio, usually so jokey, could say nothing but, 'Hermano – bro – I'm so sorry, I'm so sorry,' while Sierra burst into tears and Nina had stayed quiet so long he thought she'd hung up, till she said, 'If there's anything, anything, Milo . . . ' but then had broken off, unable to finish. It was Pablo who was the most talkative, who asked a dozen questions Emilio couldn't answer, and who ended up by saying in his usual brash way that the police were sure to be involved with the gang and the family shouldn't trust any of them, not even Castro and Alda. Emilio shouted, 'You've got no idea what you're talking about!' and slammed the phone down. Pablo rang back moments later to apologise but his words still haunted Emilio, hours later. For when all was said and done, could they *really* trust anyone? The papers were full of stories about corrupt police officers. Was Castro really the good man he appeared to be? Was the lack of progress really just a lack of progress, or was there something more sinister behind it?

A day passed. Another. Then another. And another. In all that agonising time, there was no new message from the kidnappers, or from the Federales about their investigation. The Americans called but only to 'touch base'. Everyone in the family was restless and depressed. Luz went unwillingly back to school on the second day, but the adults had taken time off work and could not seem to settle to any of their usual activities. Tío Vicente didn't even go to the cantina, and though Tía Isabel kept putting delicious food on the table, it was clear her heart wasn't in it. And when friends called to find out how they were, she put them off. Instead, she and the others spent hours at the kitchen table talking ransom money.

It was a huge worry. Emilio's grandfather had promised quite a lot of money, but even with that and Gloria's savings and everything else they could raise, they were a long way from the amount demanded. As to the insurance company, it was just as Emilio's uncle had said – they would not contribute to a ransom, only to 'some reimbursement' of money later. And the family had no idea yet if the Americans would end up contributing, or, if they did, how much they'd be prepared to give.

As to Emilio, he spent his days trying to work at the lessons his teachers had emailed to him, then giving up and trying to watch movies he could never finish, reading books he abandoned after the first few pages, starting computer games he didn't have the heart to end.

He felt he was in a horrible dream. Since he'd told his friends, they'd texted or called every day, but there was no news to give them and he did not feel like talking about other things. He missed them and he knew they would have liked to come and visit him, but their parents wouldn't let them. 'They're afraid that a kidnap might be catching,' Luz said crossly. Emilio felt bad about it but he also understood. It did feel sometimes as though he was living in quarantine, like someone sick. Nobody wanted to catch the kidnap germs. Everyone was afraid of that disease, and himself most of all.

I'm hopeless, he told himself. *Sometimes I just want to crawl into bed with the covers over my head and not talk to anyone or do anything, just go to sleep till it's all over and Mamá is back with us. But how weak and stupid is that? For the love of God, how can I help my mother if I'm weak? How can I be of any use to this family?*

Chapter 13

Finally, on the agonising fifth morning of radio silence, the next message from the kidnappers arrived. It was a stunning one.

Your request has been granted, under certain conditions which must be fulfilled exactly. A clean phone will be made available for the purpose, with place and time of the call noted in the inbox. This phone is to be obtained today, outside the Chapel of the Indians at La Villa de Guadelupe. It will be given to Gloria's son, and Gloria's son only. He is to go alone, wearing a white cap, white T-shirt and jeans, and carry a small backpack. He is to arrive at fifteen minutes to midday and wait till 1 p.m. There is to be no one following him. No one watching him. No police. You have our word he will not be harmed in any way if these conditions are followed to the letter. But failure to abide by them will result in the gravest consequences for Gloria.

There was silence for a moment while they all digested these appalling words. Then Tía Isabel burst out, 'How can they do this? How can they? There is no way we are going to put Emilio in such danger!'

'No way,' echoed her husband fiercely. 'We'll go with him.'

'I can go,' said Juanita. 'I can make sure I'm not seen. There are always crowds at La Villa.'

But Emilio found his voice at last. 'No!' he shouted. 'You read the message. You read what they said. No one else can go. I have to go on my own.'

Alda shook her head. 'It's far too dangerous. We've got to send them another message at once to say you're sick, or can't go for some reason. We simply can't allow—'

'I have to do this, I do!' cried Emilio. 'Please don't try to stop me. Please don't try to change things, or delay it. It will just make matters worse for Mamá. I know it will.' He clenched his fists. 'I want to do this for my mother. She needs me. It's the only thing I can do. They said I wouldn't be harmed. They gave their word and the basilica at La Villa is our most holy site.'

'Ha! The word of such scum is worth nothing,' growled Tío Vicente. 'Don't think that just because they've arranged this meeting in a sacred spot, they won't go back on their promise.'

Emilio drew himself up to his full height, saying defiantly, 'Then Our Lady will protect me. I'm going to do this. And you can't stop me.'

'Actually we can certainly—' began Alda, when Tía Isabel interrupted her.

'Wait. You are here to advise us, Alda,' she said, 'but not dictate what we are to do. Correct?'

'That's so,' agreed Alda.

'I am Gloria's sister. Her flesh and blood, like Emilio. I hate what these people are asking. But I do not think we can simply ignore what they say. I think we must do all we can to bring my sister back safely. And we cannot just brush aside Emilio's feelings, or his courage.' She put an arm around him. 'I know how much this has torn you up, cielito. I know how much you want to do something. But are you certain you are ready for this?'

He looked at her in grateful surprise. Nodded. 'I . . . I am.'

Tía Isabel turned to Alda. 'Would you mind giving us a little time alone as a family? We need to be united on this matter.'

Alda shrugged. 'As you wish.' And she left the room.

When she had gone, Tío Vicente said, 'Honestly, Chavelita, is that wise? She's the expert. If she says that—'

'Yes. She is the expert. But it's not her family in the firing line,' said Tía Isabel. 'These people,' she gestured towards the laptop, 'have made a concession to us, for the first time. We will be speaking to Gloria. And that will be very important. Not necessarily because of what Castro said, that it might provide a clue. I doubt that. What I do know is that we need to hear her voice. And more importantly she needs to hear ours. She needs to know we really are behind her in every way.'

Thank you, Tía Isabel, thought Emilio. She had said exactly what was in his heart.

'That phone call has to happen,' his aunt went on. 'And it's not going to if we delay or try to get more concessions out of them. I'm just as worried as any of you by what's being asked of Emilio. But I don't think we can simply say that because he is young he should not be allowed to do it.'

'I so agree! I would do it if it was you, Mamá, in Tía Gloria's place,' said Luz in a choked voice, taking her mother's hand. 'I would do it in the blink of an eye! And Papá or Juanita or the police or the President or whoever it was would never be able to stop me!'

'You little goose,' said Juanita, smiling, 'you'd have to take me with you anyway because I'm your sister and there's no way you'd leave me behind! But really, Mamá, Papá, I completely understand what you're saying.' She looked at her father for confirmation and he nodded. 'And I do understand how Emilio feels,' she went on. 'If it was me, of course I'd go at once without question. But we can't just dismiss what Alda said. I suggest we ask her if there's a way Emilio could go but also not be in as much danger, and—'

'No one can follow or watch,' said Emilio anxiously. 'You saw what they said. I'm sure they'd spot it at once.

'They wouldn't spot it if it's not a person but an electronic follower.'

'You mean, like a bug?'

'If you like. But a two-way one. You wear a concealed device which keeps you in touch with us and which transmits to us what's going on.'

'But won't they see it?'

She shook her head. 'Those things are pretty much invisible these days. So – shall I call Alda back in? Say we've agreed Emilio should go, but with the right precautions?'

There was a chorus of agreement.

When Alda came back in, she immediately said, 'Excellent solution. I was going to suggest it myself. I spoke to Raúl and he said that we'll also have people on alert close by. Very discreetly,' she hastened to add as she saw Emilio's expression. 'That's easily done in a place like La Villa, which is always swarming with people. But it is necessary. You do see that?' she went on, addressing the whole family, and when they agreed, she immediately called Castro back to arrange it all.

So that was how, a couple of hours later, Emilio found himself in a taxi on his way to La Villa, wearing an audio surveillance device concealed behind a belt buckle. The belt wasn't his; it was a custom-made one that Alda had fetched from work. She had explained how it worked. 'It's quite simple. The device transmits your conversation and all sound around you to the radio receiver at the station near the basilica, where Raúl and the others will be monitoring you the whole time. There's an embedded antenna in it which makes the transmitter's reach quite good, so they'll hear not just what's right in front of you but also along the length of the belt, to the sides and back.' She showed him a tiny switch in the buckle. 'This will activate it. Don't turn it on until you are at your destination – how about you do it after you step out of the taxi. The driver has been told to pick you up again at one p.m.'

'He's not a policeman, is he? They said that—'

'No. He's not. He's a real taxi driver. But he's one we've used before in certain situations. He's completely reliable and discreet. Now, you must also remember the code phrase you need to say if you feel threatened at all.'

He repeated it back to her: *So many people here.* It wasn't a phrase that would spook them in any way, she said. He could drop it casually in the conversation if need be. But he wasn't to hesitate if anything worried him. He had to get the backup at once, not try and play the hero. Yes, yes, he'd agreed, nervous and excited by turns as he made his farewells to his family and went downstairs with Alda to where the taxi was waiting.

He was nervous again now, as the taxi wove through the heavy traffic towards La Villa. He was in fact very nervous. What if the kidnappers realised he was wired up? What if they had been lying when they said they wouldn't harm him? What if the one who was meant to give him the phone didn't find him? His aunt had sent a short message to the kidnappers: *My nephew will be outside the Chapel of the Indians at fifteen minutes before midday and will wait till 1 p.m. He will be wearing exactly what you said.*

But how many other people might be wearing the same outfit, he thought. How could they tell one jeans-clad teenager from another?

'Oh, they'll know,' Alda had said grimly. 'They'll know exactly what you look like, and much more besides. They make that their business.'

Hope she knows what she's talking about, Emilio thought. The traffic was heavy and he began to sweat with anxiety as the taxi inched its way through the streets. He desperately wanted to tell the driver to hurry up but didn't quite dare to, so he jammed his nails into his palms to stop himself from yelling and tried to distract himself by counting the people wearing red in every colourful mural they passed by, as his father had taught him to do when he was little and couldn't wait to get somewhere. But it didn't work. Try as he might, he couldn't concentrate on that, or on any of the real-life scenes going on outside the car windows: a mariachi band playing in a square, a group of kids bashing a home-made piñata with a stick, a couple of street hawkers having an argument, an old man crossing the road on the arm of a very tall girl in very high heels, a group of policemen lounging around smoking and gossiping. All he could think of was that time was ticking away and that if the traffic didn't clear soon, they'd be too late. He prayed fervently under his breath. *Please please please, God, let us get there soon. Please please please don't let us lose this chance.*

At last they were there, with only four minutes to spare. Jumping out of the taxi after confirming a pick-up time, he activated the device and set off at a run across the huge plaza through the complex of churches towards the Chapel. The place was heaving with people. There were the usual pilgrims from all over Mexico and the world, some carrying banners, candles, statues and icons, some advancing slowly on their knees, going the last few metres to the sacred site the hard way. Emilio fought through the thick crowds of pilgrims, souvenir-sellers and foreign tourists clicking away with their cameras. He had to get to the Chapel on time!

But when he was finally there, his phone clock read twelve to twelve. He was three minutes later than his aunt's message had said. His heart was hammering in his chest. What if the kidnappers got angry that he was late, even if it was only by this little bit. *Please, Our Lady, please let it be all right*, he prayed.

Like everywhere else, the space around the Chapel was packed with people. It was very hot and his back was sweaty, so he took off the pack and laid it by his feet where he could easily see it. He waited. And waited. Midday. Fifteen past. Twenty past. Half past. He swigged the water and ate the peanuts he'd brought, trying to stay calm. He couldn't leave. He had to stay put. And yet with every minute that passed he got more and more worried.

People milled around. A few glanced at him, without much interest. A couple of beggars asked him for money and he gave them some coins. Snack- and souvenir-sellers roamed around. At one point he thought maybe one of the souvenir-sellers, a sinister-looking fellow with a lazy eye, might be his target. But the man didn't come near him, and instead headed straight for a more promising group of foreign tourists nearby, elbowing out of the way another seller, a scrawny, stringy-haired girl a little younger than Emilio, who was timidly trying to sell an assortment of very cheap medals and badly printed holy cards out of a plastic bag.

Emilio felt sorry for her, and when she came by he bought one of her medals, to her obvious surprise. She fumbled at her bag, managing to drop some of the other items in the process, so he spent a few precious seconds helping her pick them up, all the time trying to keep an eye out for the messenger. The girl thanked him shyly and walked on with her pathetic bag, trying to attract people's attention without much success. How many items would she sell today? Emilio thought, distracted for an instant from his own troubles. And how much would she make out of it even if she did? She certainly looked like someone who slept rough, and someone who didn't eat enough either. *I've never had to wonder where my next meal was coming from or where I was going to sleep at night. If I did, would I sell cheap souvenirs, or join a gang?*

The church clock struck a quarter to one, startling him from his wandering thoughts. Only fifteen minutes to go, and still the messenger hadn't come. Emilio felt sick. He'd been late by three minutes. What if the man had come during that time? What if he, Emilio, had spoiled everything? The time ticked away and away and away, and still there was no sign of anyone. As the minute hand moved closer and closer to one, Emilio's spirits sank lower and lower. Now he was convinced the messenger had come during those fatal minutes. It was his fault. He'd blown it. They wouldn't get the call from his mother. She wouldn't hear their voices . . .

Bong. The deep voice of the clock announced that it was one o'clock. His time was up. He'd failed. Crushed, he bent down to pick up his pack and put his empty water bottle in. Only then did he notice that there was something else in the bag. A phone. And it certainly wasn't his, because his was in his pocket.

The new phone, shrink-wrapped in plastic, was a cheap 'burner' pre-pay phone, the kind you could buy from street vendors and dodgy backstreet shops. Just the sort of phone the kidnappers would use. But how? No one had approached him, nobody had given him anything, he'd had the bag in his sight all the time, so how could it have—

And then it struck him. The girl. The souvenir-seller! She must have fumbled her bag deliberately, and slipped the phone into his pack when he was busy picking up her things, looking everywhere but at her. *What an idiot I am, not to spot it was her!* he thought. He had to find her, she must be a link to the gang. He knew he should call Castro, but he had no time. He had to try and find her. Grabbing his bag, he plunged through the crowd, looking in every direction to see where she might have gone. But it was hopeless. How could you see one scrawny kid among all those thousands of people? She didn't even have a white cap or a white T-shirt to flag her. But someone might have seen where she'd gone. Ay! There was the other souvenir-seller, the fellow who'd elbowed her out of the way.

'There was a girl here just now,' Emilio panted, 'a skinny little kid selling medals, did you see her?'

The man looked him up and down and said, 'Yeah, so what?'

'Please,' Emilio cried, 'it's important. Do you know her?'

The man shook his head. 'Never seen her before. She isn't a regular,' and with that he turned away to fasten on to a more promising customer.

The phone the girl had left, Emilio thought. There must be a message. Feverishly, he hit the buttons for voicemail, and for text messages. Nothing. Nothing at all. Not a clue there either. As Emilio walked numbly away to find the taxi driver, his own phone buzzed loudly in his pocket. It was Raúl Castro.

Chapter 14

'I'm sorry,' Emilio said miserably, when he'd finished telling the policeman what had happened. 'I never suspected her. I never saw her touch my bag. And afterwards when I realised – I wasn't thinking straight. I just acted on impulse. I forgot what I was meant to do. I didn't even remember to say the code phrase. If I had, maybe you could have caught her. I'm sorry.'

'What's done is done, and we can't waste time on regrets,' Castro said briskly. 'The main thing is,' he went on, 'we have the phone and the recording. Maybe we'll get something from that.'

'But there's nothing on the phone, I checked,' Emilio said.

'I know, but there are other things we might discover. For instance, there may be a fingerprint on the phone or the medal you bought.'

'But if I'd been paying attention, you could have caught one of the gang members.'

'What, the kid?' Castro shook his head. 'She won't

be a gang member. They wouldn't risk that. She'll probably be a petty thief of some sort, hired just to drop that phone in your bag. Now, you need to get away from there. Tell the driver to take you by a roundabout route to our station's address. We'll check the phone and we'll get a description from you for the identikit.'

'But what about the phone call with the gang?' said Emilio. 'What if they say it's got to happen really soon?'

'It won't. They'll know they have to give you time to arrange for the Americans to come too. Now then, we'll be as quick as we can at the station and then you'll be driven straight home. Your family's waiting for you.'

✦

At the police station, Castro introduced a man as the police sketch artist. Emilio tried to remember something useful about the girl. 'She had a thin face, dark eyes, she wasn't pretty, exactly, because she was too thin and kind of grubby too – but not bad-looking either, if you know what I mean. No distinguishing features, I mean no scars, moles, tattoos, birthmarks, nothing like that. She was dressed in a blue T-shirt with a logo on it, just an old Mexico City souvenir thing, a denim skirt, and scuffed sandals. Her hair was black, stringy, tied back with an elastic.' He looked at the sketch artist, who had been busy with a drawing program on the computer. 'I'm sorry. That's not much, is it?'

'No. It's good. Don't you worry,' said Castro. 'Have a look at what Rafael here has come up with and tell us if you think it's a fair likeness.'

Emilio peered at the picture on screen. 'Um, I'm not sure. It kind of looks like her, I suppose.'

'Now then, that medal,' said Castro. 'We'll need that too. Her prints may be on it. If she's in the database they'll show up.' He handed Emilio a plastic bag. 'Drop it in here. Your prints will be on it already, but that's okay, we can quickly eliminate them. And here's the phone back.'

Emilio looked at him. 'But don't you need to . . . '

'It's already been examined. No prints on it at all, completely clean. These people are cunning as foxes,' said Castro. 'I'm sure the message will arrive today but at a time of their choosing.' He got up. 'We'd better get you and that phone home at once.'

The route the taxi took brought him past his actual home, the home he hadn't seen since the day his mother was taken, and a great longing suddenly seized him to retrieve something of his mother's, anything to remind him of her, to make her feel closer.

'Please, can you stop at this address?' he asked the driver.

'I'm not sure if—' began the driver.

'It's okay,' said Emilio hurriedly, 'I'll only be a few minutes, just to pick up a few clothes and DVDs, no one will mind. Please.'

The driver raised his eyebrows. 'Okay then. But be quick.'

'I will,' said Emilio fervently, and jumping out of the cab, he hastened to key in the security code and raced into the building. He hoped Señor Santiago wouldn't be hanging about; he didn't feel like having a long conversation. But the caretaker's door was closed with the TV going behind it, so he got into the lift and up to his own apartment without being spotted.

It was weird, turning the key and coming in. It was home and yet now he was only visiting. He'd felt safe and happy here but now it carried the atmosphere of a day that would be forever burned into his memory. He took a deep breath. No time to stand here brooding.

He flung a few clothes and DVDs into a bag, just so there'd be no boring questions. Then he went into his mother's room. It was neat and tidy, the way she always kept it. He looked around. A photo. That would be a good thing to have. That picture, there, on his mother's dressing table, of the three of them, his mother, his father, himself, around the time of his tenth birthday. They'd gone for a beach holiday at Veracruz, the last holiday they'd taken together, just a few weeks before his father was killed in the car crash. It had been a wonderful holiday. And everyone looked so happy. It was the last time he could remember his mother looking really happy, he thought, a lump coming into his throat.

He had just put the photo carefully away among his clothes in the bag when his eye was caught by something else on the table. Lying beside a gold bangle with Aztec symbols and a pair of emerald earrings that had once belonged to Gloria's mother was a little silver and turquoise brooch in the shape of a heart. It had been his father's first serious present to his mother, when they were courting. Emilio knew the story well. He'd loved it when he was little but found it embarrassing later. He stared at the brooch, his pulse racing as a strange idea flashed into his mind. *My little heart,* his mother had written in her letter. *Think of my little heart, my Emilio.* He'd thought it odd. What if she'd intended not an appeal to her sister to think about Emilio, her 'coranzito mio', *but a direct message to Emilio himself?* 'Think of my little heart.' What she'd meant was *her heart brooch.*

But why? Why would she? What was so special about the brooch? He took it out of the jeweller's box lined with white satin, and turned it over. On the back were the words his father had had engraved for her: 'My heart for you, always.'

Tears pricked at Emilio's eyes. Yes, this little heart meant a lot to his mother. But why, in such danger as she was, would she send Emilio a message about it? He could hardly send it to her. Could she have intended that the brooch should be sold to help with the ransom money? But if that was so, why hadn't she included the rest of the jewellery in the message? The heart brooch was very pretty but the earrings and bangle were much more valuable. Yet it was the only thing she'd specifically mentioned. He couldn't work it out. But he knew that he had to take it with him. It meant something, he was sure of it. Perhaps Tía Isabel would know. Or the police.

But he'd better get a move on now or the driver would be getting worried. Putting the brooch back in its box, he grabbed his bag and went out of the apartment, locking the door carefully behind him.

Chapter 15

Emilio was almost at the flat when the phone beeped twice. New text message.

Today 19.00 h.

That was it. That meant seven in the evening. Five hours from now. In five hours he would at last hear his mother's voice, even if he couldn't speak to her.

He clicked back to the details of the message, hoping against hope they might have been careless enough to leave a trail. But of course they hadn't. Aside from time and date, 'Private number' was all it said on the screen.

The taxi drew up outside the block of flats. The driver said, 'Will you be all right or do you want me to come inside with you?'

'I'm fine,' said Emilio, jumping out of the cab. Looking up at the window, he could see Luz framed there, watching the street. She saw him and waved. He was about to put in the security number when an elderly lady came out. He knew her. She was Señora Valdez, who lived a floor down from the Torres family.

'Oh Emilio! Oh my dear,' she said, laying a hand on his arm. 'I read about your poor mother. So awful. I'm so sorry.'

'Thank you, Señora,' he said, a little impatiently. He wanted to get upstairs, and show the others the text message.

'Please tell your aunt that if there's anything I can do to help, she's only got to ask.'

'Thank you. I will.'

'It's the curse of greed,' she said sadly, 'the curse of greed that's destroying our poor country. All people think about is money. No one knows right from wrong any more.'

He wished she'd stop talking, but he couldn't tell an old person to be quiet.

'I hope you're getting proper help,' she went on.

He nodded. By now she'd know about Alda, but only as the Nicaraguan cousin. And it had to stay that way.

'In the old days there were bad men too,' she said, 'but at least they had some kind of honour. A code of some sort. These days, they have none. The drugs have scrambled their morals as well as their brains. As to the police, well, if they're not corrupt they know nothing and they're incompetent. We live in bad days.'

'I'm sorry,' he said desperately, 'but I must go.'

She eyed his bag. 'You'll be staying here a while longer, then.'

He nodded.

'But surely you shouldn't be out by yourself,' she cried. 'Why are you—'

'I just had to run an errand,' he said hastily. 'I'm sorry, but I really have to go.' Finally he made his escape, taking the stairs two at a time back to his aunt and uncle's flat.

'We were starting to get worried about you,' said Tía Isabel when she opened the door. She saw the bag in his hand. 'What's that?'

'Just some clothes I picked up from our place—'

'Madre di Dios, Emilio, why do that? Raúl told us you were coming straight back,' she scolded, but he gabbled, 'It's okay, I'll tell you about it later, but Tía, Tía, the message – it's come!'

Her face froze. She said, 'When?'

'When I was in the taxi.'

'No, I mean when will the call be?'

'Tonight. Seven.'

She put her hand out and he gave her the phone. She looked at the message without speaking, then hurried to the living room where the others were waiting, and he followed her.

But he didn't get a chance to tell everyone his idea about the 'little heart' till later. He and Luz had been banished while phone discussions were going on with the Americans. He brought out the brooch from his pocket, and told Luz his idea.

'What do you think?' he finished. 'It's not really valuable. So why would she have mentioned it?'

Luz turned it between thumb and forefinger. 'Maybe to remind herself of you?'

'That isn't like her.'

'I know what you mean,' said Luz. She stared down

at the little blue-and-silver heart as though she thought that looking at it hard enough would make it yield up its secret to her. 'Maybe it's some sort of a clue? Like the medal, I mean.'

'What sort of clue?' cried Emilio. 'I've racked my brains and I can't come up with anything.'

'Heart,' said Luz seriously, 'little heart. Love token. Silver. Turquoise.'

'Have you gone loca, cousin?'

'No, I'm not going mad,' said Luz with dignity, 'I'm just trying out ideas. Your mother must have meant something by it, or she wouldn't have mentioned it.'

'I don't even know if I'm imagining it anyway,' sighed Emilio. 'Maybe she really did just mean to call me by that name. Maybe I—'

'No,' said Luz firmly. 'I'm sure you're right. Tía Gloria was trying to send you a message.'

'Then what was it?'

They both started as there was a knock on the door. It was Juanita. 'Emilio, do you—' She saw the brooch lying on the bed. 'What's that?'

'It's Tía Gloria's,' burst out Luz before Emilio could speak, 'and Emilio worked out that was what Tía Gloria meant in her letter when she said about a little heart and so that's why he brought it here!'

Juanita looked astonished. 'What are you talking about?'

'It's a clue. Like the medal, and—'

'That's just an idea,' Emilio interrupted. 'It's probably nothing.' And he explained.

Juanita looked at him, then at the brooch. She said, 'Wait a moment. I'll get Alda. She should hear this.'

So Emilio had to tell his idea a third time, to Alda and his aunt and uncle. By the time he'd finished it sounded threadbare, barely credible even to him. The brooch had been handled by all five of them, every millimetre of it scrutinised, the engraving read and re-read, every memory of it talked over – and still there was no clue. And then Alda, who had been deep in thought, said, 'Did you just bring it loose in your pocket?'

'No,' said Emilio, 'in its box,' and he handed it to her. She opened it and peeled up the white satin backing to look underneath. Nothing. She checked the lid, inside and out. Nothing. On the underside of the box, though, was a label with a name on it – the name of the shop where Emilio's father had bought it, all those years ago. But the print was faded, practically rubbed off. Alda peered closely at it. 'I think it starts with F – or is that a P?'

'No, not P,' said Tía Isabel suddenly. 'F. Flor. Flor de las Joyas, Flower of Jewels, that's what it was called. I remember my sister telling me. It's long gone now, that shop, but it was one of her favourites, and I think Jorge had heard that—'

She never finished her sentence, for with a muttered exclamation, Alda raced out of the room, dialling as she went.

Chapter 16

'**Señor Castro believes this is** a real breakthrough,' said Alda a short while later. Her eyes were shining. 'We know at last who we are dealing with.'

'But are you sure?' said Tía Isabel.

'Yes.' And she told them about an arrest a few months ago, of a gang leader who went by the name of el Capitán, the Captain. 'He's connected to a Sinaloa drug cartel, and most members of his gang hail from there, but he's been operating semi-independently in Mexico City for about six years. We've been after him for a while but he was protected by corrupt police, and it was only when one of them was nabbed for something else, and flipped and gave us information, that we were able to set up a sting which netted us both el Capitán and two or three of his top men. Thing is, though el Capitán is in jail right now, and his trade's been severely disrupted, a number of his gang remain at large. One of them's a young woman, who's reputed to be as lethal as the men, though we know very little about her apart from the name she goes by.'

'Flor,' breathed Emilio.

'Yes. In full, actually, she's known as Flor de la Noche – Flower of the Night. Your mother must have overheard her name at some stage. Señor Castro thinks it likely she was one of the so-called nuns who abducted your mother.'

Tío Vicente shook his head. 'Gloria took a bit of a chance. We might not have understood what she was getting at.'

'*We* didn't, Chente,' observed his wife tartly. 'It was Emilio.'

'I didn't get it at first either. It was just I thought it odd that she called me corazoncito,' said Emilio. He felt so proud of his brave, resourceful mother. 'When she calls, can we tell her that – that we got her message?'

'That would not be wise,' said Alda.

'Alda's right, Milo,' said Juanita, and his aunt and uncle echoed her words. Only Luz said nothing. From the look in her eyes Emilio knew she was thinking the same thing as he was. His mother should be told. She had to know her message had got through. And he would do it. He just had to do it in a way that nobody would suspect. He had to think . . . His eye fell on the brooch, and he picked it up again, stroking the silver and blue, turning it over. And an idea came to him.

Time passed. Seven o'clock drew near. The Americans – Sellers a wiry, dark-haired, blue-eyed man in his forties, and Taylor, an older, more suave type, with sleek silver hair and a smart suit – had arrived, driven in an unmarked police car by one of Castro's team dressed as a chauffeur. Listening devices had been set up to link the car to the flat and record the call. Everyone was on edge but trying not to be. Tía Isabel handed around fresh crispy churros and horchatas, a refreshing drink made with ground almonds and milk, while Tío Vicente and Juanita made nervous smalltalk, to which Sellers responded in excellent Spanish and Taylor hardly at all. Emilio sat mutely next to an equally silent Luz on the sofa, and all he could think of as the clock hand crawled towards the hour was *I must make sure Mamá knows*. As the time got closer, seven minutes to seven, six, five, four, everyone fell silent. Everyone was watching the phone on the table, the phone the skinny little girl had delivered to Emilio at the basilica. And then, right as the clock touched seven—

A phone rang. Loudly. But not the phone on the table. Not the phone that everyone was watching as though they were birds hypnotised by a snake. Someone's mobile.

'For God's sake!' shouted Tía Isabel. 'Switch that thing off!'

'I'm sorry,' said Tío Vicente. 'I meant to, sorry, I'll do it right now and . . . ' He trailed off, the colour draining from his face.

'What is it?' cried Tía Isabel, as the Americans looked at each other, puzzled.

'Private number. No one I know has a private number,' Tío Vicente whispered.

The same question was on all their faces, as they looked at Alda. Alda said, 'Answer it. Now.'

Tío Vicente pressed the answer button. 'Who – who's there?'

'Hola, Vicente Torres,' said a tinny voice over the loudspeaker, so distorted by interference that it was impossible even to tell if it was male or female. 'Now pass the phone to your wife, as she is clearly the boss.'

Tío Vicente flushed, but before he could say anything, Tía Isabel touched him gently on the shoulder, murmuring, 'Don't let it matter, mi amor, my love.' She held out her hand for the phone.

'Isabel Torres here,' she said, as everyone listened tensely. 'I thought the call was to be on the phone you provided.'

'We changed our minds. The Americans are here?' said the distorted voice.

'Yes.' She glanced at Sellers and Taylor. Sellers mouthed, 'Would you like us to say something?' She shook her head.

'Good. Then they and you will hear our proposal from Gloria's own lips.' There was a clunk, a rustle, and the voice suddenly cut out, leaving the family looking at each other, bewildered and not a little chilled. But that was forgotten as quite suddenly a familiar voice came on the line, faraway, but unmistakable: the voice of Emilio's mother.

'Isabel – are you there?'

'Yes I am, mi hermana querida, my darling sister,' said Tía Isabel, her voice shaking. 'Are you – how are you keeping?'

'I am as well as may be expected,' said Gloria.

Emilio's heart raced. His skin felt clammy. He hardly noticed Luz's hand creeping into his. 'And you – how are you, Chavelita?' his mother went on. 'How is the family?'

'Okay, querida mia,' said Tía Isabel, 'but thinking of you all the time.'

'How is my little heart, my Emilio?'

'I am well. But I miss you. My heart for you always, Mamá,' Emilio shouted, so that she'd hear. There. He'd said it. He'd said what was written on the back of the silver heart. She'd know what it meant. And those bastards who held her wouldn't have a clue.

'My heart to you too, my Milo,' she said, and there was a new lilt in her voice, so that he knew for sure that not only had she heard but she'd understood.

A painful feeling gripped in Emilio's chest. He was so glad he'd said it. He was so glad he could hear his mother's voice. And yet he felt a sharp pain too, his eyes stung with tears and his throat was choked with words he could not say.

'Sister,' his mother went on, 'we don't have much time, and I must put a proposal to you and to our American partners which is to the satisfaction of – of the people here. Having considered the financial information you provided, and as a gesture of good faith, they have been kind enough to agree to a special arrangement.' Her voice was toneless as she said the last sentence, and they all knew she did not at all mean 'kind'. 'They will accept two million pesos in cash.'

Everyone looked at each other in stunned relief and astonishment. It was less than a third of the original demand. Still a large sum, but not completely out of reach. But before Tía Isabel could speak, Emilio's mother went on quickly, 'But they want something else as well. Holiday South owns shares in a hotel in Veracruz. They want those shares.'

'What?' The Americans had started up from their seats. Taylor hissed, 'Are they crazy? We'll never . . . '

But his friend, Señor Sellers, flapped a hand at him to be quiet. 'Ask Señora Lopez to repeat that,' he said to Tía Isabel.

She did so, and Gloria repeated what she'd said, adding, 'I am so very sorry. I do not know how they – how they knew . . . ' A pause, then she went on, 'But it's their condition for agreeing to a – to a lower cash component. I – I am to tell you that this is the final offer.' Gloria's voice went dry, as though she were reciting a lawyer's letter, learned by rote. 'No further negotiation will be entered into. You must all agree to this deal without attempting to change it in any way or it will be null and void, and' – her voice faltered – 'you know what that means.'

A cold shiver rippled up Emilio's back.

'There must be no police involved,' Gloria continued. Everyone looked at Alda, who shook her head. *The gang must not know she is police*, Emilio thought. That was something. His mother went on, 'You will soon receive detailed instructions by email as to how everything is to be done. As soon as the demands are met, I will be released. What is your response?'

Tía Isabel glanced at the Americans. Taylor opened his mouth, but Sellers cut him off. 'Tell her we agree.'

'But . . . ' began the other American.

Sellers put a finger to his lips. 'Tell her we agree,' he repeated in a louder voice.

Relief and astonishment flooded through Emilio. Did the American really mean what he said? Or was he only pretending, playing for time?

'Yes,' said Tía Isabel into the phone. 'Yes, Gloria. We agree, on the whole deal. All of us, the family, and Señors Sellers and Taylor too.'

'Then I—' began Gloria Torres, but then her voice cut out and was replaced by the hateful tinny voice.

'There. That wasn't hard, was it?'

'Please,' said Tía Isabel shakily, 'let us say goodnight to Gloria.'

'No need,' said the tinny voice. 'She'll have a good night, knowing her family and friends would never try to betray her, won't she? Won't she?' it hectored, when Emilio's aunt didn't answer quickly enough.

'Of – of course,' said Tía Isabel quickly. After a pause, she said softly, 'And thank you, for letting us speak to her. For giving us hope.'

There was a silence, though they could all hear the person at the other end breathing. Then the voice said, 'You'll hear from us,' and the call ended as abruptly as it had begun.

Chapter 17

For a moment, no one spoke. Then Alda said, 'Well! I understand what you were trying to do, Señora Torres, but these people are rarely to be moved by appeals to their better natures, and now you have given them exactly what they want, and they feel they hold all the cards—'

'Well, don't they?' snapped Tío Vicente. 'We want to save Gloria's life, after all, and they have it in their hands! Until we can get her back, who cares if they think they have it all over us?'

Before Alda could answer, Tía Isabel said to the Americans, 'We understand that last demand is impossible for you, and . . . '

'You can't mean that, Tía,' burst out Emilio.

Sellers said, 'Wait a moment. It's not impossible, Señora Torres.'

'You can't mean to say you really would be prepared to do that! But we can't expect that. It's not right. Not fair. We will somehow have to try and change their minds,' said Tía Isabel, sadly.

'You heard your sister,' said Sellers. 'This is their final demand.'

'But maybe they don't mean that.' She turned to Alda. 'What do you think?'

'I think that these people know what they're doing,' she replied. 'And that they have excellent information. What is the hotel you own in Veracruz, Señor?' she asked, turning to Sellers.

'It's called Cielo del Sur, Southern Sky,' answered the American. 'And we aren't the outright owners, we just own shares.'

'But a substantial number?'

'Close to a half,' said Sellers, ignoring Taylor's glare.

'They'd be worth a good deal?'

'Yes. ' He frowned. 'But I don't understand. If that's what they wanted, why didn't they kidnap *me*?'

Emilio thought, He's right. And a bitterness came surging through him. If only – if only it *had* been Señor Sellers they'd taken! It was a bad thing to think, he knew that, especially when the American had been so kind. But he couldn't help it.

'You are American, Señor,' said Alda. 'To kidnap an American is problematic. It would bring too much heat on them from both here and beyond the border. This way, they get double the value at half the risk. I'm sorry to put it that way,' she added, seeing the family wince, 'but that's how these people think.'

'But why then didn't they make that demand first?' said Tía Isabel.

'It's likely they didn't know about the hotel till

afterwards. They must have done their research since then.'

'Señora Lopez knew about it of course,' said Taylor, and flushed a little at the looks everyone, including Sellers, turned on him then. 'Not that I mean anything by that. I'm real sorry for Señora Lopez and all that, but there's no way in the world we're handing those so-and-sos our hotel.'

'Oh no. They'll *think* they're getting what they asked for,' said Sellers, with a grim smile. 'There are ways we can do this that will make it look as though we're complying. That's all we need to do.'

'I would advise against trying to play games with these people,' said Alda. 'We can stall them maybe, but until we know who they are, I suggest . . . '

'Oh, as for you,' barked Tío Vicente, 'all you want to know is who you're dealing with, but all we want is to get Gloria home safe!'

'That's not fair, Papá,' said Juanita. 'Alda's goal is just the same as ours. And she's doing all she can to help us.'

'Oh, I know that, I know that and we're grateful, Alda, really we are, but you lot are no closer to finding these bastardos really, are you?' said Emilio's uncle, ignoring warning looks from his wife and elder daughter. 'Okay, so you may know now what gang's involved – but as you don't know where they are, that doesn't help, does it? Nobody's going to tell you a thing.'

'There's that policeman, the corrupt one, who helped put them in jail,' said his wife. 'Maybe he'll have an idea where they might be.'

Something flickered in Alda's eyes. 'Mmm,' was all she said.

'By the look of your face, I'd say that was highly unlikely,' said Tío Vicente. 'If that guy is even alive any more.'

'I can't reveal . . . We don't care about him or any other supposed informer,' interrupted Tío Vincente, 'you know damn well we don't have time for possibles and maybes. What we do know is that this was the final offer. No more negotiations. You heard.'

'Yes, but Papá,' said Juanita, 'they said that before. And yet they changed their minds.'

At that moment, Alda's phone rang. It was Raúl Castro. She filled him in rapidly on what had been said, and he told them he had good news. It had taken a little while, but the call had been traced. And it hadn't been made from a cellphone, but from a street payphone. 'There's a car heading to that precise location right now,' he said.

'How is that possible?' said Emilio's aunt.

There was a short, confused silence. 'A car has been dispatched to—' Castro began.

'No. No. What I mean is, if they made the call from a payphone, then they must have been there with Gloria. Someone would have noticed.'

'Yes. Exactly. That's what we think. Even if they're gone by now – which is likely – someone may well have noticed them. And even if they haven't, the payphone's on a busy street, not far from various shops. Someone may have a camera installed. It's being checked right now.'

'You don't understand. What I meant,' said Tía Isabel, 'is why would they use a payphone when it was likely they could be spotted forcing Gloria to say what she had to say? That seems very careless.'

'That's because it is,' said the policeman. 'Remember, this is a gang without a leader. Without even the top lieutenants. Junior people are running this operation. They make mistakes more easily. And they don't have the smarts of el Capitán or his top people.'

'Surely he'd be directing every aspect from jail?'

'He'd try. But it's difficult to do so. He can't control it to the same level as he would if he were free.'

'Where does that leave us?'

'It leaves us much closer to locating them,' Castro said smoothly. 'Don't worry, Señora. I will be in touch again as soon as there is any more news. Meanwhile, make sure to contact me as soon as you receive the email with their "instructions".'

A little later, Emilio's grandfather rang. When he heard about the new demand, he immediately said he'd make arrangements to give half of the cash ransom. 'I'll arrange for it to be transferred to Gloria's account first thing tomorrow,' he added, and would not listen to any word of thanks. 'It's normal, just normal. And tell those snails of Federales to get themselves moving,' he growled.

At least he was in agreement with us there, Emilio thought. That was about the only thing they agreed on, though, as the discussions between the family and the

Americans went on well into the night, with no email arriving from the kidnappers. How were the Americans going to give the impression that they were doing what was demanded, while not actually giving over their shares? Emilio had no idea, for he and Luz were not allowed to listen in and had to go to bed. He was really scared, though he tried not to show it. Alda had said you shouldn't play games with these people. Emilio was terribly afraid she was right. The kidnappers would know if they'd been tricked. And they'd take it out on his mother. Maybe Alda was right and they should just try to stall them, somehow. But that too was dangerous – what if they lost patience? But how could you trust what Alda said, either? Sure, she had helped them a lot. Sure, she wanted it all to end well. Sure, and her background meant she understood what kidnap victims went through. But she still wasn't personally, emotionally involved, and that made a big difference.

He slept badly again that night, tossing and turning as he relived the conversation with his mother, hearing her voice again and again, trying to think over and over whether she had sent yet another coded message. For the life of him, he couldn't work it out. Most of what she'd said had been straightforward – either the words she'd had to parrot for the kidnappers, or the few ordinary words she'd been able to exchange before that. Of course she'd also managed to ask the question, and he'd been able to answer her, without arousing the suspicions of the wicked people who held her. But everything else had been what you might expect. Nothing was mysterious or stood out. Or did it? Again and again his mind went round and round like a rat in a cage until finally he fell into a heavy and unrefreshing sleep.

The email still hadn't arrived next morning. Hours went by and then it was afternoon and still it hadn't come. Neither had any news from Raúl Castro. Presumably police inquiries as to who might have been at the payphone had failed to yield any useful information. Alda said that because the payphone in question didn't use coins but telephone cards, it was possible that the card used by the kidnappers could be traced through its pin number, which might be in the machine's databank. But searching that would take time. As usual. So much about this was about waiting. Waiting. Hoping. Fearing. Waiting. Waiting . . .

There was no news from the Americans either. They had gone to 'prepare papers', according to Tía Isabel. She wouldn't say any more. The family spent much of the day huddled around the computer, fuelled by massive amounts of caldo de pollo, chicken soup, and chilli quesos, cheesy spicy dip with fresh tortillas. They combed the internet for information on the gang leader, el Capitán, real name Juán Andrés Medina, who came from Culiacán, the capital of Sinaloa province, one of the provinces most dominated by the cartels. His was a 'connected' gang, which of course meant connected to the big local cartel. He was from a well-off family, and in Mexico City he had owned a couple of 'legitimate' businesses – a security firm and a restaurant – into which, secretly, went his drug-trade income, so that it looked as though he was just an ordinary successful businessman. These had closed about a year before his arrest. But it was rumoured he'd afterwards bought into a tourist resort in Cancún, through a frontman. And one of the articles also mentioned that there was a young woman nicknamed Flor de la Noche in his gang, and it was hinted she had carried out some of the gang's killings.

'Medina might be in prison awaiting trial,' Tío Vicente observed in disgust, 'but the scum has a luxurious room and can get pretty much anything he wants. As to his lieutenants, they do not seem to be too worried either. Their boss is looking after them, even in prison.'

Alda nodded. 'None of the gang would do anything without his knowledge, whether inside or outside of prison. His reach is still there. The change of plan has to be his idea. And if the rumours are true, and he's bought into tourist resorts, then dishonestly acquiring a hotel in Veracruz would be right up his alley.' She gave a grim smile. 'He is clearly intending to reinvent himself as a hotel mogul. It's not uncommon. More than one flash hotel has been developed with drug money.'

'But this mongrel takes it one step further and plans to just help himself,' snarled Tío Vicente. 'Why work after all, even in their vile business, if you can just take what's not yours? And don't tell me it's because he's gone without in his life. Why does he need more?'

'Greed is always hungry,' said Alda quietly.

Tía Isabel had been deep in thought, and now she said, 'That child at La Villa – the little pickpocket – it's a long shot, but I wonder if perhaps Padre Benitez might know something about her?' She turned to Alda. 'He's our parish priest, but has also done a lot of work in the area around La Villa, especially with orphans . . . I know he hates the drug trade and what it's done to families and to our country. And he said he'd help us in any way he could. I'd like to call him.'

'Do as you wish,' said Alda, 'but be discreet.'

'Of course,' said Tío Vicente, 'what do you take us for?'

So they called Padre Benitez, just saying they needed his help, and he came round shortly after. He sat with them in the living room, sipping on café con crème, listening intently to Emilio's description of what had happened at La Villa. Following Alda's advice, they had not told him the full story – 'for his own protection as much as yours,' she'd explained. 'As we all know, even priests are not immune to the violence of the drug war. More than twenty have been killed in the last few years because they tried to protect people against the drug cartels, or worked with teenage victims.' They'd all gone quiet after that little speech. None of them wanted the Padre to suffer.

After Emilio finished, Padre Benitez was silent a moment, then said, 'Did you notice if she had a local accent, or one from elsewhere?'

Emilio thought about it. She hadn't said much. 'I wasn't paying much attention,' he said. 'But I'm pretty sure she did not have a Mexico City accent.'

'Think carefully. If it wasn't from here, where else could it have been from?'

Emilio pondered, thinking about people he knew who came from other parts of Mexico. His grandfather, for instance, had the accent of Mérida. Sierra's mother came from Yucatán, and had that kind of accent, while Alda's real accent was northern, but her fake one was Nicaraguan. And Señora Valdez, downstairs – she came from the Guatemalan border and her accent was sing-song. 'Yes,' he said, remembering. 'That girl, she sounded a bit Guatemalan. But not really. I mean, maybe she comes from one of the states that border Guatemala.'

'Are you sure?' asked the priest.

'Not one hundred per cent certain. But I really do think so.'

'Good. Then that gives me something to work with.' Padre Benitez got up. 'I'll start making enquiries right away.'

The day wore on. Nothing much happened for hours. There was no email from the kidnappers. Castro did not call. Señor Sellers called, but only to say that he would be visiting first thing next morning. Emilio Skyped with his friends for a short while, played cards with his cousins and thought endlessly about what had happened at La Villa and whether there was anything he had overlooked. But he couldn't think of a thing. It looked to him as though the kidnappers had so far planned everything very well. If it hadn't been for his mother's quick wits, in fact, nobody would have known a single thing about who they were or how they'd done it.

Finally, at around eight, Raúl Castro rang again. He had good and bad news. There'd been no useable fingerprints found on the medal. But on the payphone lead, there'd been an unexpected development. Castro said that there had been no sighting of any suspicious activity at the payphone, but a nearby shopkeeper had assured him that only people on their own had called from that phone during the day. Nobody had come in pairs or threes, he said. And so Castro had come up with a new theory: that Gloria herself had not been there at all but had spoken from captivity, patched in on a cellphone the kidnapper had held up close to the receiver, which would explain the clunking and the faraway sound.

'The shopkeeper was asked if by any chance he'd observed such a thing but he hadn't,' went on Castro. 'Not surprisingly, as the kidnapper's back would have been turned to him. We asked him to try and describe as many people as he could remember who had used the payphone that day. We're lucky: he's an observant man and he did remember a few people. There may be something in there that we can compare against descriptions of known members of el Capitán's gang.'

Tía Isabel raised an eyebrow. 'Then let's hope something good comes of it,' she said.

Chapter 18

A disturbing thing happened next morning, not long before the next email from the kidnappers finally arrived. Their downstairs neighbor Señora Valdez knocked on their door to tell them she'd had a strange phone call.

'I'm sorry to interrupt your Saturday morning,' she said, as she sat at the table drinking a cup of coffee and eating some cinnamon bizcocha, 'but I thought you should know at once. A nicely-spoken young lady rang up to say she was from some travel company that had wonderful special offers for people under thirty living in this area. Did I have a child or grandchild of that age residing with me? she asked. I said no, but that my grandson was twenty-four and he lived not all that far away. Then she asked me if any of my neighbours had family members of that age, and I said yes, and she then said she was looking at a list of names, and did I know if for instance the Torres family had family in that age bracket residing with them? Well, I was a bit surprised by that, but I thought I could do you all a good turn, so I said yes, there was a daughter of that age, and then the young woman said, was that all? And I said, well, there's a nephew, but he's too young, he's only thirteen and oh yes, there's a cousin staying there at the moment too, she's from Nicaragua, she's in her twenties. And then they said, can you give me her name? And that's when I really smelled a rat, and I said that I didn't talk to snoops from Immigration, and hung up.' She looked around the table with an anxious expression. 'I hope I haven't caused you any trouble.'

'Er, what?' said a bemused Tía Isabel, shooting an anxious glance at Alda.

With a broad smile, and an even broader Nicaraguan accent, Alda said, 'Don't worry, Señora. That immigration official who tried to trick you, she is barking up the wrong tree. I'm not an illegal. My papers are all in order. I wasn't going to visit my Mexican family for the first time without making quite sure I wouldn't run into any trouble!'

'Oh, of course you wouldn't,' said the old lady with a sigh of relief. 'The cheek of these people! Pretending to be from a travel company indeed! Silly of me to have fallen for it at first, that's all.'

'Not at all, not at all,' said Tío Vicente. 'Anyone might have done so.'

'Thank you very much for telling us,' said Tía Isabel. 'That was very kind.'

'What are neighbours for?' said the old lady, smiling. 'Another biscuit?' she responded as Luz offered her the plate. 'Well, why not?'

It wasn't until the Señora was well out of earshot, on her way down the stairs, that Alda was able to call Castro with the news and discuss what had happened. Everyone was somewhat uneasy; it was obviously one of the kidnappers, quite possibly the shadowy Flor herself, who had made the phone call. It seemed they had their suspicions about Alda. On the other hand, there was a definite upside to it. The old lady's rebuke to the 'snoop from Immigration', and the way Alda had played up to it, was all in their favour. It bolstered Alda's cover story not only among the neighbours but beyond, and would probably allay the kidnappers' suspicion.

Raúl Castro agreed. 'Still, none of you should relax your guard. Watch your tongues, all of you, especially the young ones.'

Why especially us? Emilio thought, bristling, as the policeman hung up. *As if Luz and I have been wagging our tongues all over town!*

Just then Juanita gave an exclamation that brought them all running to the computer screen. The kidnappers' email had come. What it said made Emilio's heart sink.

All paperwork on the hotel shares to be completed and scanned into a message by 14.00 hours today. When we have checked all is in order, we will advise on next step. Meanwhile, prepare ransom money in units of 20-, 50- and 100-peso notes only, new polymer notes only.

Tío Vicente looked grim. 'Two o'clock! That's just two hours away! And Sellers rang this morning to say the papers weren't ready yet!'

113

'We'll call him,' snapped Tía Isabel. She picked up the phone. *Please please please,* Emilio thought, *please let it be okay . . .*

And it was. 'I'll expedite it. We'll have all the documents by midday, come what may,' the American said, his voice coming steady and calm over the speakerphone. 'Hang in there, my friends. It'll soon be over.'

'But are you sure – are you sure your plan will work?' said Tía Isabel, with a break in her voice.

Emilio didn't know exactly what stratagem the Americans were using to make it look as if they were actually handing over their shares. He only knew they wouldn't be handing them over.

'Don't worry, Señora Torres. Our lawyer's drawn it all up to look totally official. It will fool them, I can guarantee you that.'

They could only hope he was right. Because if he wasn't – it didn't bear thinking about. But after he rang off they sent a message back in reply to the kidnappers, agreeing to all the terms.

Alda rang Castro to tell him, and he did not react well, bawling her out. 'You should have put them off for a while,' he said. 'We're not ready – and if the bluff doesn't work, then the Señora is dead. You should have waited. You should have asked my advice first!'

'I'm sorry, sir,' she said, white-lipped, 'but I can't force the family to—'

'Put the Señora on the phone,' said Castro testily, and when Tía Isabel came on the line, he scolded her, saying that he had begun to develop what he called a 'channel' to the gang members in jail, and that this 'amateur bluff' might render that useless.

'I don't see why it would,' said Tía Isabel coldly, 'and we're not asking you to approve. For us, Agent Castro, it's very simple. We want to get my sister back safe and sound. That's the beginning and end of it.'

'Of course,' said Castro, softening his tone, 'but you must understand that there are many aspects to consider in this situation.'

'Not for us there aren't,' said Tía Isabel, and she handed the phone back to Alda and walked off without a word.

Emilio and Luz went after her and found her sitting on her bed with her head in her hands, weeping silently. They each put an arm around her, and soon Luz was crying too. Emilio choked with anger and grief but couldn't cry; the tears just burned in his throat and his eyes. *They don't know what it's like,* he thought, *people like Castro. They don't understand. If it was their family, what would they do?* But he had no answer to that, any more than he could understand why this evil had been visited on his family rather than someone else's. This man who called himself 'the Captain', this woman who called herself 'the Flower of the Night', they were human beings and yet they and their kind acted like tigers in the jungle, preying on innocents who crossed their path.

***

At eleven, the phone rang, and they all started towards it. But it wasn't Señor Sellers. It was the priest, Padre

115

Benitez. 'I'm sorry that it's taken me so long,' he said, 'but I've got a name for you. Evita. Evita Delgado. I was told that she's a pickpocket who sometimes works around La Villa, and that originally she's from Tabasco. I'm afraid I couldn't find out where she lives, or where she might be now, but I thought it was something you could pass on to the investigators.' He would not accept any thanks for his help, saying only that he wished he could have done more. 'If I could have found the child myself, I might have persuaded her to help you. But I was afraid that if I asked too many questions, those who hired her might hear of it and then her life would be in danger.'

'Who cares about that little thief's life?' snapped Tío Vicente when his wife told them what the priest had said. 'The Padre should think more of poor Gloria's.'

'He is,' said Tía Isabel, exasperated, 'but he's a priest, not a judge, and besides, can't you see, you tonto, that if we lose the girl, we also lose an important lead?'

Emilio caught Luz's eye. She smiled. *Parents!* her glance said. *So embarrassing!* Emilio smiled back, a little sadly. How he wished he too could roll his eyes at an antic of his mother's!

Castro received the Padre's information rather coolly. 'We'll look into it,' was all he said. But at least he refrained from giving them another lecture about amateurs. Just as well, thought Emilio, seeing his aunt's fiercely determined expression.

Nobody felt much like lunch, but Tía Isabel heated up the remains of last night's pork stew and made fresh tortillas and a salad. Emilio ate without interest. Like the others, he kept watching the clock. Half past twelve. A quarter past one. Half past. Only half an hour to go till the kidnappers' deadline, and Sellers still had not appeared.

It had just gone eight minutes to two when the street-door buzzer rang. It was Sellers. He came panting up the steps, red-faced and sweaty. 'Sorry. So sorry. The final documents didn't come through from my lawyer on the fax till one-twenty-five, and then I scanned them in and put them on a USB stick and came as quick as I could, but the taxi got stuck in a traffic jam. I had to abandon it and run all the rest of the way.'

'Let's get this into our computer, then,' said Juanita, nearly snatching the USB from him. Emilio's heart was in his mouth as she rapidly copied the files, attached them to a message in the Draft box and added a very brief cover note. *Documents as promised.* By the time this was all securely done, it was four minutes to two.

'And now to wait,' said Tío Vicente. 'Again. Waiting on the good grace of scum. It makes my blood boil.'

Nobody said anything to that. They just kept watching the computer, watching the Draft box. As if that would do any good. As if it might show the face of their enemy and give them a clue, an advantage, something.

They all jumped when the phone rang. It was Castro. 'We've got the Delgado girl on file,' he said. 'She's been picked up once before. I've got people out looking for her right now. But don't get your hopes up too much.

117

It might turn out she's not the girl Emilio saw. These types of kids are not exactly uncommon. And even if she is the one, she likely knows nothing.'

'Well, isn't he the little ray of sunshine?' said Emilio's uncle ironically when the policeman rang off. And for once, Tía Isabel didn't reprove him. 'Señor Sellers,' she said, turning to the American, 'we'd like to thank you for everything you're doing for us.'

'Wait to thank me till we know it's worked,' said the American. He smiled. 'And please, ma'am, won't you stop calling me Señor Sellers? Makes me feel like my own father. My name's Steve, and I'd be honoured if you might call me that.'

Tía Isabel smiled back. 'Very well, Steve. But you must stop calling me ma'am, then, and do us the honour of using our names. Mine's Isabel, my husband's is Vicente, and my eldest daughter's is Juanita. The kids you already know. And you must allow this family to thank you properly, once this is over. You didn't have to do any of this – we'd have quite understood if you didn't want to be involved.'

'Look, Isabel, fact is, I kinda feel responsible for what happened to Gloria – yeah, I know it wasn't my fault, but if she hadn't been associated with me maybe none of this would've happened. And I'll feel happier if I can actually do something for her. Now don't you worry. It'll all work out.'

Emilio hoped he was right.

Chapter 19

'**Do you know what date** it is the day after tomorrow, Milo?' asked Luz suddenly, as they sat in her room watching a DVD that night.

He shook his head.

'It'll be the first of November,' she said.

Of course. The first of November was Día de los Inocentes, Day of the Innocents, in memory of children who have died, followed by Día de los Muertos, Day of the Dead, honouring people who died as adults. Before his father's death Emilio had enjoyed the festival, and later had founds its traditions comforting. Every November, he'd gone to Mérida with his grandfather to visit his father's grave, bringing gifts, telling him stories of what was going on. But this year, everything was different, and he couldn't help feeling the date was a bad omen.

Luz saw his expression. 'Sorry, I didn't mean to—'

'It's okay,' said Emilio, with an effort. For a few more moments he stared at the movie without taking any of it in, feeling he needed to move, but knowing that if he did

Luz would feel bad, and then she'd go on about it and he wouldn't be able to bear it. So he forced himself to stay there until at last the credits rolled and he was able to get up. He said, 'I'd better go to bed. I'm exhausted.'

'Yes,' said Luz, darting a glance at him. 'Me too.'

The adults were sitting around the kitchen table when he went through to his room. They smiled and wished him good night but the strain on all their faces told him that a good night was unlikely for any of them. Until they got a message from the kidnappers saying the papers were in order, they would not know if they'd done the right or wrong thing with this 'amateur bluff'. If Emilio's mother suffered as a result, then they'd have that on their conscience. Nobody said it, but everyone thought it.

Emilio woke suddenly and looked at his phone. Nine o'clock! Oh no! He'd slept right through his alarm. Scrambling into his clothes, he went out into the kitchen. Everyone else was up, even Luz. They all looked solemn. And there was an extra person at the table. Raúl Castro.

'What's happened?' Emilio cried, fearing the worst.

'Very early this morning we picked up Evita Delgado – that chiquita, that little girl from the basilica.'

Emilio sat down suddenly. 'So Padre Benitez was right! It was *her*!'

'Fits your description, yes.'

'But how – where was she?'

'She was caught being light-fingered outside a flash nightclub and was beaten up by club security. One of the patrons called the police, luckily, before any lasting damage was done. She's in the hospital now. And we've been talking to her.' He gave a rather sour smile. 'Or rather, we've been trying to.'

'She won't say anything?'

'Nothing about what we want. We've offered her a deal – we cut her loose if she'll tell us who hired her for the handover of the phone. She won't know their real name, of course, only what they chose to tell her. But it's a start. I've told her that if she doesn't talk, her case will go straight to the magistrate and she's sure to cop a longer period in detention as she's a repeat offender. She's scared of that. I know she is. But—'

'But she's more scared of the people who hired her,' said Emilio.

Castro shook his head. 'I don't think so. It's just that people like her don't talk to the police.'

'Then how—'

'I think it's worth trying another tack. That's why I've come. She may speak to someone from the family. Your aunt has agreed to have a go.'

'I want to come too,' said Emilio at once.

'Milo, I don't think—'

'Please,' he said. 'I'm the one she's met. I spoke to her. I bought one of her medals. I'm about her age. She might speak to me. Please let me try.' Seeing they were still hesitating, he added, 'And besides, I'll be able to say for sure it was her.'

Tía Isabel looked at Castro, who nodded. 'Very well. We'll leave as soon as you're ready.'

All the way to the hospital, Emilio's anger was rising as he thought about Evita Delgado's part in the kidnap plot. He'd shout at her, shake her, he thought, force her to tell him what she knew. But his feelings changed when he first glimpsed her through the window of the small room. She looked awful. There was a bandage around her head, she had a big black eye, and cuts and bruises on her face and her skinny arms. Huddled in the narrow hospital bed, she was staring at a TV without appearing to be really watching it.

Castro looked at him. 'Is that the girl you saw at La Villa?'

Emilio nodded. 'It's her, for sure.'

His aunt said, 'She's so tiny.'

'She's twelve,' Castro said. Emilio's heart clenched. She was the same age as Luz. 'She's an orphan,' Castro went on. 'A cousin from here took her in – he was a rather dodgy character, and was shot in a gang incident a year or so ago. She's been alone on the streets since then.'

'Poor child,' breathed Tía Isabel. 'The people who beat her—'

'They'd say they were within their rights. After all, she's a thief. It wasn't the first time she'd been seen hanging about there.' Then his tone softened. 'Look, I've made sure she can stay for a day or two at least. She'll be fed and looked after. And she can help herself, depending on what she does now. Either she goes back to juvenile prison or she goes free.'

'Back to the streets?'

'Well, that depends. Your Padre Benitez. He might help. They tell me he's got connections to a good orphanage. But she's not the only one in need, you understand. Now, shall we go in?'

She didn't look at them as they came in. Castro said, 'Evita, there are some people who want to talk to you.'

'Evita,' said Tía Isabel gently, 'we really need your help. Please.'

The girl didn't reply. Instead she stared fixedly at the TV, on which a rerun of a popular cartoon, *Oggy y las cucarachas*, was playing at full blast. As a little kid, Emilio had loved the antics of the lazy blue cat Oggy in his eternal battles with three clever cockroaches, called Joey, Dee Dee and Markey.

Castro said, 'I'm going to turn it off. Can't hear ourselves think here.'

Evita said nothing, though her hands clenched on the sheet. But Emilio said, 'Please don't. This is a really good episode. I'd like to see it again if that's okay.'

Tía Isabel understood at once, Castro an instant later. He shrugged, and with a nod at Emilio, he followed Tía Isabel out of the room. Emilio and Evita were left alone.

Emilio pulled out the plastic chair that stood in the corner of the room, and sat where he'd be facing the TV, not looking at her. He knew it was important that he did not spook her. And though it was a weird situation to be in, he was kind of enjoying watching the cartoon anyway, laughing again at the silliness of it. It wasn't until the final music died away and an ad came on that he said, 'What's on next, do you know?'

This time she did look at him. She shook her head.

'This is an old TV so they won't have a menu, but I can look up the list of programs on my phone. It's Cartoon Network, right?'

She nodded, and watched him as his fingers scrolled rapidly over the screen of his phone. 'Hey, it's *Johnny Bravo*,' he said. 'Do you like that?'

She shrugged. 'It's okay,' she muttered, speaking for the first time.

'Well, maybe you want to watch some more *Oggy*? They've got lots of episodes on YouTube. I can get them on my phone.'

Her eyes lit up. 'Okay,' she said. So he turned down the sound on the TV and brought up an episode of Oggy, which they watched together, he laughing, she much more serious. *But maybe it hurts the poor chica to laugh right now*, Emilio thought, *what with all those bruises*.

They finished watching that one and he was about to bring up another when she said, 'You are the boy from La Villa.'

'Yes,' he said, and his heart began to race. 'My name is Emilio. Emilio Mendoza Lopez.'

'You can ask me if you like, Emilio,' she said, looking at the screen of the phone and not at him.

His heart raced faster. 'The – the person who asked you to give me the phone – did you know them?'

'No,' she said.

'Did they give you a name?'

'No,' she said. 'He just gave me money.'

'Please,' he said. 'Can you describe him?'

She looked away.

'Please,' he begged. 'Please. My mother – my mother has been missing for two weeks now and I am so afraid for her—'

There was a silence. Then she said, seemingly not answering the question, 'I saw him again last night.'

Bewildered, he said, 'What?

She pointed to her bruises. 'I saw him at the place where they gave me this.'

Emilio stared. 'You mean – he was one of the security guards who bashed you?'

She shook her head. 'No.' Her eyes flashed. 'But he saw them do it. And he didn't care. He and his girlfriend, they just walked into the nightclub. It was someone else who called the cops.'

'He and his girlfriend?' repeated Emilio.

'Hanging all over him,' said Evita scornfully.

'Oh my God,' said Emilio. 'Are you sure? I mean, that it was him?'

'Yes.'

'Evita,' he said, 'will you—'

She nodded.

'Can I go and get my aunt? And Señor Castro?'

'Not him. Her, yes.'

'Okay.' He looked at her. 'Thank you,' he said. 'Thank you so much.'

She shrugged, and jerked her head at his phone. 'I want to watch *Oggy* again now.'

'Okay,' he said, handing it to her. 'You watch whatever you like, Evita,' and he raced off to find his aunt.

Chapter 20

The nightclub turned over its security-camera footage to the police, insisting that only Emilio and his aunt be in the hospital room with Evita when she identified the man she had seen. Emilio stared at the image. The man hadn't troubled to hide his face from the camera – obviously he felt utterly safe. He looked to be in his late twenties, with the nuggety build of a boxer under the trendy clothes, and there was a San Malverde tattoo clearly to be seen on his bare forearm, suggesting he might have been one of the kidnap team.

The young woman with him was pretty, with long, wavy, light brown hair, wearing an outfit that showed off her curvy figure, plus high heels and a diamond heart on a chain around her neck. Evita said she'd never seen her before. But was she involved too?, Emilio wondered. Could she even be Flor? She didn't look like a lethal gangster. But then, why would she? Even the man, apart from that tattoo, looked like any young guy out with his girl, having a good time.

Castro told them that police records had come up with an identity for the man. Four years ago police had been called to a gym a few streets away from Lopez Travel after a violent quarrel between the manager and a client who gave his name as Miguel Luna Esposito. As to the girl, she was not associated with the gym in any way – nobody there recognised her – and face recognition showed she wasn't in the criminal records either.

From the manager the police learned that Esposito had been working at the time for a private security firm called Mirasol Security – the security firm that Medina, el Capitán, had owned until a couple of years ago. So the link to the gang was there too.

Now Emilio and his aunt worried about Evita. 'She's a street kid and wary as a lizard,' said Tía Isabel to Castro, 'but she is still only a child, after all.'

'If the gang finds out that she gave us information,' said Emilio, 'they'll punish her. Bash her or even kill her.'

'You can rest assured we'll keep her safe,' said the policeman. 'And she's under age. She can't be forced to be a witness at any trial, so the gang will never know a thing. And afterwards – well, you heard what Padre Benitez said. That orphanage he works for will take her, as soon as she's released from hospital.'

'Have you told Evita about that?' Emilio asked Castro.

'No. Best not to. But she'll be okay once she's there.'

Emilio wasn't sure about that. 'Tía,' he said to his

aunt, when Castro had left, 'could we – er – maybe – could Evita come and stay with *us*?'

His aunt looked at him in surprise. 'No, Emilio, it's too dangerous. For her as much as us. Remember that phone call Señora Valdez got about Alda. They're watching. They will know who Evita is. If they see her there with us, they'll know she's talked.'

He knew that was true, but he still felt bad, so he spent most of the money in his bank account on a smart-phone for Evita, complete with a six-month pre-paid SIM card so that she could watch YouTube whenever she wanted. He gave it to her that very day. 'It's for me?' she repeated. 'For *me*?'

He nodded.

'Show me how it works,' she ordered. So he showed her everything about the phone and what you could do with it, and then he added impulsively, 'You can call or text me if you like, any time.' He put his number in the contact list, with just 'Milo' as the identifier, as a precaution. She met his eyes and nodded, once. Then she looked down at the phone and began playing with the buttons and he knew she wanted to be left alone with her new toy.

A spurt of the old anger rose in him. She'd not thanked him, any more than she'd said she was sorry that she'd helped the kidnappers, even if in a small way. But the anger didn't last. This skinny stray was what her hard life had made her, he reasoned, and needed help not punishment. But there was nothing else he could do for her right now. He'd done all he could, Tía Isabel assured him. More than he should, Tío Vicente grumbled when he heard. But Juanita and Luz understood how he felt, and so did Alda, who afterwards came to tell him that like Padre Benitez, she'd also try to keep an eye on what happened to Evita in the future.

Chapter 21

The next morning, they received the email they'd been hoping for. Clearly the kidnappers had no idea they'd been tricked about the hotel shares, because though they didn't even mention the papers being 'in order', they gave their usual arrogant instructions. Alda said, 'These people will never say thank you or please or even give you the merest indication they are pleased with what you've done, but take it from me, everything has worked. And they think they hold all the cards.'

They read the email several times.

These are your next steps. Cash to be delivered tonight. Midnight, San Gregorio cemetery, exact place to be texted. Entire sum to be in one bag. All the family to be there. But only family. No release for Gloria until our messenger safely back with money. Any police or others attempt to stop our messenger, any attempt to vary anything, and Gloria dies. We will be watching. And you will never see us.

'It's going to be very difficult to spot anything suspicious there,' said Juanita. 'It's so huge! And there'll be countless people praying and partying at relatives' graves. They know what they're doing, this gang.'

'Yes,' nodded Alda. 'You heard what Lieutenant Castro said. Even if he had the men and budget to stake out the entire place, which he doesn't, it would be difficult.'

'Soon we're going to hand over almost all our family savings. And our American friends have to play a very dangerous game with their property,' said Emilio's uncle. 'Yet there's no guarantee of Gloria's release. Seems to me the kidnappers have snatched their cards back.'

'And Señor Castro says he hasn't made any more progress on finding Esposito and Flor, or discovering more about their connection with el Capitán's gang,' said Alda.

It was a frantic day and yet one that seemed to unfold as slowly as an old man's curse. In the morning Emilio and Luz had to stay at home while the adults, including Alda and Juanita, went out to collect the money from the bank manager. Just before she went out, Alda asked the two cousins to keep an eye on things. 'Both on the laptop and the phone, and call me at once if anything changes.' she said. 'Okay?'

Emilio and Luz nodded. Alda smiled and gave them a thumbs-up. 'It'll be fine, you'll see,' she said, and went out.

Emilio and Luz looked at each other. 'Hope she's right,' said Luz. 'Emilio, what do you think – I mean, what do you think we're going to see in San Gregorio?'

Emilio's skin crawled. *I can imagine all too many*

things, he thought, *but I'm certainly not going to say them out loud.* 'No idea,' he snapped.

'I mean, how do you think they're going to collect the money? Do you think they'll send someone like Evita again?'

'How should I know?' said Emilio. 'Please, Luz,' he added, as his cousin opened her mouth again, 'I really don't feel like talking. Let's watch some TV instead, okay?'

'Okay,' said Luz, shrugging. They sat side by side watching TV, with the laptop open in front of them. Or at least Luz watched TV. Emilio couldn't settle. Jumping up from the sofa, he paced around and around the flat. *I feel like a rat on a wheel,* he thought, *going mad. I can't wait till midnight but I'm so scared of it too. Because Mamá might be released then. But also she might not. She might even be killed.* He tried to keep out the fearful and excited voices in his head by drowning them with loud music in his headphones, but even through his favourite songs he could hear the voices and it made him feel as though he was being pursued by demons.

Out of the window, he could see people passing by dressed in holiday clothes, and streams of cars heading for the Plaza a short distance away, where there were going to be parades and a fair and all kinds of celebrations. The cars were decorated with images of dancing skeleton couples in top hats and frilly dresses, and skeletons drinking beer, and skeleton cowboys on horseback, and skeleton musicians playing guitar, and skeletons doing all kinds of things, and it was as though they were mocking him, as if their bare skulls and bony cheeks shook with laughter at what was happening to him.

At one stage, he locked the bathroom door, sat on the floor, closed his eyes and tried to concentrate on a game his father and he had played when he was younger. It was the game of telepathy. You had to try and 'see' what the other person was thinking by closing your eyes and concentrating really hard on them, in your mind. Emilio wasn't much good at it. But his father had been excellent, he had 'seen' a few times what Emilio was thinking. At least, that's what Emilio had thought when he was small. He'd been impressed, and a little frightened too. He must never lie to his father, he'd thought, because his father would know for sure. Now Emilio suspected that his father had merely made accurate guesses, because he was an adult and adults had been children once and so could work out more easily what a child might be thinking. He thought, *Maybe it'll work if I concentrate really hard on Mamá. I might be able to send her a thought somehow, so that she can feel she's not alone, and will soon be safe home with us—*

He concentrated and concentrated but it was as though she was in a grey fog and he couldn't get through. It was a stupid idea, he told himself angrily as he got up and splashed water on his face, hardly realising he'd been crying.

Suddenly his phone rang, and he grabbed it, his heart hammering. But it wasn't the kidnappers. It was Pablo. 'Just calling to see how things are going, Milo,' his friend said.

'How do you think they are?' Emilio shouted. 'Are you an idiot?' He clicked the phone off, only to call back a few seconds later to apologise.

'It's okay, hermano,' said Pablo awkwardly. 'I get it, we all get it.'

Emilio could hear street noise in the background and he knew Pablo must be out somewhere, enjoying the holiday with his family and friends. A terrible longing filled him then. If only he was Pablo. If only he was Sergio. Or any other of his friends, anyone other than himself. Then he could be out there having a good time, feeling sorry for a friend going through a bad time, sure, but not actually having to go through that bad time.

Not long after, Emilio's grandfather called. 'I've been lighting candles at the church, Milo,' he told Emilio. 'For both your Papá and your Mamá.' *Mamá's not dead yet, Abuelo!,* Emilio wanted to yell, even though he knew his grandfather hadn't meant it that way. The candles for Gloria were for her safe return, just as they'd lit candles at the church here the other day. They weren't for the repose of her soul. But still, it *was* the Day of the Dead, and so a bad omen, and he wished his abuelo hadn't said it, and wished too that the old man hadn't sounded, well, really like an old man, much older and more tired than Emilio had ever heard him, with a croaky voice rather than his usual sharp, firm tone. And when he first called, he had said to Tía Isabel, 'I want to hear my grandson's voice.' That, too, was unlike him. Emilio heard himself promising to come down south with his mother 'when she is well enough'. Which brought him back to his fevered thoughts about midnight, and the endless waiting.

The adults were back just before lunch, Juanita carrying the money in the big, flowery-skull canvas shoulderbag that she'd bought from a street stall the year before. It was exactly the sort of thing you could carry on the Day of the Dead without attracting any attention; and the money in it, though it was so much, hardly made more than a small hump in it. But though the bag was put away in a cupboard out of sight during lunch, its presence hovered among them like a malevolent ghost. In it were pretty much all Gloria's savings, a large slice of her father-in-law's money, and some of his aunt's and uncle's too. It meant a big financial sacrifice for all of them. More than that, those notes, those coloured pieces of plastic, represented, horribly, the price of Gloria's freedom, the value of her *life*. It was hateful. Shameful. How could people think this way? Did they have no heart, no soul at all?

Afternoon crept along, and evening. Castro called. He had some news, not about Esposito or Flor or their fellow gang members still at large but about a conversation overheard at the jail where their leader was being held. Medina had told an associate that 'the parcel' had been delivered and that 'our friends' would now 'have to deliver as promised'. It sounded as though the hotel shares that they'd demanded from the Americans were intended as payment for a favour yet to be fulfilled by the cartel. Security had been tightened at the prison in case the favour involved some kind of attack or breakout there, but what the conversation had suggested was that Medina was in touch with his gang on the outside, and had almost certainly authorised the kidnapping.

'Not much use to us,' said Tío Vicente, after Castro had rung off. Emilio thought the same. They had battled every step of the way, trying to outguess their enemies, trying to get clues, trying to win a bit of ground and claw back a bit of hope. But now there was only the final confrontation when they would have to face the unknown in the candle-lit city of the dead.

Chapter 22

It was a quarter to midnight, at San Gregorio cemetery. The family had got there by eleven o'clock, just in case, and brought every mobile phone they had with them, including the 'burner' Evita had delivered. But there had been no word from the kidnappers, and they'd been walking among the decorated, candle-lit graves, carrying the bunches of big orange marigolds traditional for this day and trying to look as though they had somewhere to go. But nearly all their relatives had come from outside Mexico City and were buried elsewhere. Tío Vicente had one cousin buried here, 'but my side of the family never really got on with his,' he explained, 'and I don't think he'd welcome me here at all.'

The graveyard on this night was a weird mixture of noise and silence, golden lights alternating with pools of deep shadow, the scent of incense and perfume mingling with an underlying faint earthy mustiness, the warmth of thousands of candles meeting the cold of autumnal midnight. Emilio knew this was the time of night when the dead were supposed to break free of the bonds of the afterlife and mingle with the living, and their families were waiting for them. Beautiful temporary altars had been created at each attended grave, decorated with all kinds of things: colourful garlands of flowers, photos and paintings of the dead, holy pictures, candy skulls, dolls in elaborate costumes, painted shells, bright bits of lace, and candles, many candles. At some graves, mariachi bands performed cheerful tunes to welcome the spirits or rowdy family parties raised glasses and talked and laughed; at others, relatives sat quietly, blankets around their shoulders, keeping vigil for their loved ones. But none of their faces could be seen until you were close up, and then they might look at you briefly, or nod and say something in greeting, or else simply ignore your presence. Some graves were unattended, though even most of these were decorated with flowered altars and candles that flickered over the headstones, throwing odd shadows. There were a few obvious foreign tourists, too, wandering with wide eyes, cameras at the ready.

At one stage, Luz's hand crept into Emilio's, and he was glad of its warmth, for so much about him felt cold even though he was wearing his fleecy hooded jacket. They didn't speak, though the adults talked in an undertone to each other. Alda was with them. 'I'm supposed to be a cousin!' she told them sharply when Tía Isabel had said she shouldn't come. Thanks to Señora Valdez, the kidnappers had bought the cover story of the 'Nicaraguan cousin'. Coming to the graveyard with the family would strengthen that.

Ten minutes to midnight. Five. Castro was somewhere in the cemetery with one of his men, but keeping well away from the family. He'd given orders that none of his men was to approach the kidnappers' messenger or make any arrests till Gloria was released, but to maintain surveillance. As to the kidnappers, *They are probably here already*, Emilio thought. *All those watchers, and we can see no one.*

Or Gloria will die. That stark phrase from the kidnappers' last message kept going around in his head. And in this place between death and life, he kept seeing himself in the future, walking down just such a row, not aimlessly waiting, but with a clear destination – his mother's grave. He hated the thought, tried to push it away from him, but it kept coming back, like a persistent pop-up ad on a computer screen.

He jumped, and dropped Luz's hand. His cellphone was vibrating. 'It's them!'

'What?'

He pulled out the phone. All he could see was 'Private number'.

The message said, *Hinojosa, Maria.*

And that was it. It was exactly midnight.

He raced to the others and showed them, without a word. Alda said, 'That's the place.' His uncle said, 'But how are we supposed to know where, there's no map.' Juanita said, 'We'll have to go back to the entrance and ask a caretaker.' But his aunt said nothing. She just kept walking, straight ahead, and stopped at a grave where an old couple, he large and silent under a bobble hat, she small and neat in a scarf, the pair of them muffled up almost to the eyebrows against the cold, and well wrapped in stripy woollen ponchos, were patiently keeping vigil. Emilio was the first to follow her, the others hurrying after.

The old woman proved helpful. 'Oh yes, I know where Maria Hinojosa is planted,' she said, 'she's not far from our own son's grave here.' The old man stayed morosely quiet and didn't even look at them. They thanked her profusely, Tía Isabel slipping her some coins – 'for candles,' she said – and hastened in the direction the old lady had indicated.

It was tucked away in a corner, near some bushes. There was only a small headstone and it was old, dating from the 1920s, with the writing almost faded away. They could only just make out the name and the date. It was not flowered or candled, and indeed looked rather neglected. That must have been why the kidnappers had chosen it.

Just then came another cellphone ping. Not his, but his aunt's, this time. *Leave the bag and go home*, said the private number.

They looked around. There was no one nearby, apart from the old couple, and they'd returned to their own concerns. And there seemed to be no one lurking in the bushes, though they could hardly check. Then Tía Isabel's phone pinged again. *Do it. Now.*

'They're here, close by. They can see us,' whispered Alda. 'Do just what they say.'

Juanita, who'd been carrying the bag, placed it carefully behind the headstone.

'What if someone else finds it first?' Tía Isabel said anxiously. 'Everyone's hard-won savings gone, and for nothing.'

'They won't,' said Alda.

Emilio said, 'Please, we have to go. We have to go now.'

'But we can't just—' began Juanita.

'We can and we must. Emilio's right,' said Alda. 'Their messenger will only pick up the money when we've gone. The sooner we do this, the sooner Gloria will be released. Trust me. I've seen this before.'

There was no more argument. The family walked back the way they'd come, without looking back. As he followed, Emilio could feel a prickle on the back of his neck, like a cold wind nudging at his skin. *They're here*, he thought. *Somewhere. Maybe they're hiding in the bushes, or maybe they're heading to the grave now.* Knots of people passed them as they walked along, and he kept thinking, *It could be one of them.* A mariachi band came towards them, and he wondered if it wasn't just another disguise for the kidnappers. And then suddenly, as they were nearly back at the entrance gate, something came into his mind, something he'd half seen and not made sense of till then, and he couldn't help giving a small gasp.

'What is it?' said Luz, beside him.

'Nothing. Just a stitch.'

But it wasn't nothing, and it wasn't a stitch either. What he'd half seen was an image of the headstone near where the old couple sat. The first time, when they'd stopped to ask directions, he hadn't seen it, because the old man's body had obscured it. And on the way back he'd glimpsed it only fleetingly. The last date on that headstone – it was 1930-something, he was sure of it. So how could it possibly be where the old couple's son was buried? Even if they were a hundred years old, the dates didn't work.

But they weren't a hundred years old, he thought. They weren't real old people, any more than they'd been real nuns. They were part of the kidnap gang.

His heart pounded. His skin felt clammy. He couldn't say anything to anyone. He mustn't. Not till his mother was safely back. The hair on the back of his neck prickled more than ever. He wanted those people caught. He wanted them punished. But just for this night, hc had to let them get away. If they didn't, his mother would die.

It was a silent drive back to the flat. No one felt like talking. Alda was texting, presumably to Castro. Emilio couldn't see what she was writing. But she hadn't seen what he had. Nobody had. He was sure of that. Or was he? Anxiety flooded through him. What if right now police were storming through the cemetery, racing to get their hands on the 'old couple'? But no, he was sure they weren't. Anxiety was followed by wild hope. They'd done what the kidnappers wanted, in every way. Maybe when they got back to the flat, his mother would be there, waiting on the doorstep. He could almost see her there, tired and pale but so glad to be alive. So glad to be back with him, and with the family. He'd hug her and hug her and not let the police come near her with their questions. He'd not let anybody bother her. He'd make up his bed in the spare room with fresh sheets and she could sleep there. She'd need to sleep. In the two weeks those creatures had held her, she'd probably hardly slept. They'd probably deliberately kept her awake, those . . . He clenched his fists in his lap. He hated them worse than ever, now. They had turned him into a coward.

When they returned, she wasn't back, of course. He hadn't really expected her to be, he'd known that was just wishful thinking. It was still a blow, but he soon forgot it, for when they switched on the laptop – just in case, Alda said – there was a message.

Gloria will be released tomorrow.

Chapter 23

It was nearly 2 a.m. when they got back from the cemetery, but the message made sleep impossible for the family. Everyone was too jumpy. Alda was the only one who could face going to bed. 'There's nothing else we here can do for the moment,' she said. She'd briefed Castro fully on what had happened. He and his colleague had not had time to get to the Hinojosa grave in time to see who had taken the bag. Listening to this, Emilio felt a squirm of unease. He knew he should speak out about 'the old couple'. But he couldn't. He just couldn't. Until his mother was safely back with them, he would keep his mouth shut. He didn't care about the kidnappers. He didn't care about the police investigation. He just wanted his mother back.

As the night wore on, Tía Isabel made dozens of fresh tortillas and gallons of coffee and chocolate, and they ate and drank with blankets around their shoulders against the late-night chill and played cards and lit candles and prayed for Gloria's safe return and for the repose of the souls of their departed, including Emilio's father. It was a very small and very sober tribute to the festival they were missing, and it helped to calm them all somewhat. Luz eventually fell asleep at the table with her head pillowed on her arms, and her father carried her gently to her room, but Emilio stayed wide awake, his mind buzzing with anticipation and anxiety, checking from time to time to see if there had been any further message. But there was none.

Five o'clock came. Six. And then at 6.15 precisely, the downstairs buzzer rang. They all rushed to the intercom, but Emilio got there first. A voice said, 'Parcel delivery.'

All the blood rushed out of Emilio's face. He tried to speak, but couldn't. His aunt took the phone from him. 'Who is this?'

'Parcel downstairs,' said the voice, and cut out.

Emilio ran for the door. Tía Isabel said, 'Wait, we have to—' But he didn't stop. Fumbling with the locks, he pulled open the door and vaulted down the stairs to the bottom floor, where the mailboxes were. There was nothing there; but when he pulled open the street door, he found—

No, not his mother, but a little box, wrapped in newspaper and addressed to 'the Lopez/Torres family'. The disappointment was so sickening that he nearly threw up. An instant later, as he remembered some of the things he'd read about families being sent ears or fingers or other body parts of victims, he imagined what might be in that box, and he really was sick, throwing up much of what he'd eaten that night.

'Milo, Milo, come inside.' Juanita's hand was gentle on his shoulder. Emilio looked up, his throat raw, his eyes red. Alda was with his cousin, her normally neat clothes rumpled as if she'd slept in them. She picked up the little box. She said, 'I think it's a key. I can hear it rattling.'

Emilio was ashamed, about imagining things, about throwing up, about how shaky his limbs were, about how helpless he felt. Wiping a hand across his mouth, he nodded mutely, and followed the two young women back into the flat.

It was just as Alda had said. The little box held a key. There was a printed note taped to it. An address which proved to be an abandoned building located in the neighbourhood of La Villa de Guadalupe.

Things moved very fast after that. Castro was informed and immediately arranged a car to take the family to the place. Not Emilio and Luz, though – he was categorical about that, and for once all the others agreed. It was much too dangerous, they said, and no matter how Emilio argued, it didn't change things. A young policewoman – not Alda, who went with the others – was left with them, for protection they were told, but Emilio suspected it was just as much to make sure they didn't disobey orders and leave.

Anger at being treated like a child soon gave way to gnawing fear. What if the kidnappers were playing yet another of their games? What if his mother wasn't at that address? Much worse, what if she was, but not—no, he wouldn't think that. He wouldn't. He couldn't. He'd made Tía Isabel promise she'd call him as soon as they had found his mother, but the time seemed so long, so long, and he couldn't concentrate on anything, pacing up and down while Luz and the policewoman played cards. *How can they?* he thought. Clutching his mother's 'little heart' in his hand, he paced, and prayed under his breath, promising God all kinds of things if only his mother could come home safe. *I'll never try to get out of Mass, I'll never laugh again at the catechism teacher's upcountry accent, I'll study more, I won't draw rude cartoons of the teachers, please, if you'll only help us, I'll do anything! I'll even give up my iPod for Lent, well at least for Holy Week, I promise, God, please!*

When he was in the kitchen getting a drink of water, his phone rang. He jumped to answer it. But it wasn't his aunt. It was Evita.

'I've just seen the man,' she said, without preamble.

'What?' Emilio had no idea what she was talking about. Then he realised she must be speaking about Esposito, the man who'd sold her the phone. The one who'd taken Flor to the nightclub. But he didn't care about that man, not right now. 'Look, I'm waiting for a call – it's really—'

'He's at a plant stall in Mercado Jamaica,' she said, ignoring his interruption. 'But he's not buying.'

'Oh,' said Emilio weakly, wondering briefly what Evita was doing at the plant market. Wasn't the orphanage supposed to have picked her up when she came out of hospital?

'He's selling,' Evita said. 'I can see him. But he can't see me.'

'Oh. Good.' Luz and the young policewoman had heard the phone and come into the kitchen. He mouthed, *It's not them.*

'I thought you and your tía might want to know,' Evita said.

'Oh. Thanks.' He felt bad about shuffling her off quickly, but he was really desperate to have the phone line free. 'I really have to go and—'

'Is your mamá okay?' The simple question took him by surprise.

He gulped. 'We – we hope so.'

'I will pray for her.'

'Thank you,' he whispered. He struggled to regain his composure. 'We – we will speak later. I promise.'

'Okay. I send you now a picture of the stall,' she said abruptly, and rang off. An instant later a picture message came through. Obviously Evita hadn't yet mastered the phone camera very well, or she was trying to zoom in from a distance, because it was a bit blurry. But he sent the picture through to Alda, with an explanation. She'd pass it on to Castro. And, feeling guilty, he texted Evita, too. *Thank you. Speak soon. Hope you are enjoying YouTube.* A text came back almost at once. *Yes!*

He must not forget about her, he thought. Once it was all over, he had to try and help her. Right now, though, he couldn't think of anything else than what might be happening at that abandoned building. Why hadn't they called yet?

Half an hour later the call he'd been longing for finally came through. 'Milo, your mamá querida, your darling mother's here. Oh my God,' said his aunt, her words tumbling over each other. 'Oh my God, cielito . . . '

His stomach lurched with terror. 'What's wrong? Is she – is she . . . '

'She's alive, Milo, she's alive – oh yes, I'm with her now.'

'Can I speak to her? Please. Please.'

'No. No, Milo. She's not – she's not awake. She's in a coma. They drugged her, you see. She – she's being taken to hospital. I'm with her in the ambulance.' His aunt's voice was shaking. 'I won't leave her, don't you worry.'

He shouted, 'I want to be there, where are you taking her, I have to be there!'

'Yes, yes, of course you must, cielito, of course you will, they're sending a car now to get you – tell Luz to come too – oh Milo, Milo, I can't believe it – I still can't . . . ' She sounded as young as Juanita, almost as young as Luz, and suddenly Emilio felt the last of his self-control disappear, swept away by an overwhelming rush of pent-up feelings. He was crying, with happiness, with anxiety, with all the wild unleashed stress of this terrible fortnight. He hugged Luz, who was crying too, and even Alda looked tearful and told them over and over again that it would be all right, everything would be all right now.

When Emilio first saw his mother lying unconscious in the hospital bed, so grey and drawn, with livid bruises and cuts both old and new on her face and body, he thought, *No it* won't *be all right!* She wasn't at all well, the nurses said; she'd been given a high dose of some very powerful sedatives on top of having been poorly fed, beaten more than once, and kept in a room so small 'it might as well have been a box,' said Tía Isabel.

'Those bastards,' said Tío Vicente, clenching his fists, 'they'll pay, don't you worry, they'll pay dearly for what they've done . . . '

Emilio didn't care about the bastards, not now, not yet. All he cared about was that his mother should get well. He did not want to let her out of his sight. He was utterly exhausted but he thought that if he closed his eyes she might disappear again. He didn't say that to anyone, of course. The family could stay for a while, the nurses said, as long as they did not get in the way. She was being well looked after, medically. And there was a policeman sitting outside the room, just in case. At one stage, Castro came in to find out exactly what Evita had said when she phoned from the plant market, and Emilio answered all the questions as well as he could with his mind not really on it. All he could see was his mother's still face and dark hair against the white pillow, and her chest so still under the hospital sheets, and the fear rose in him, hissing, *What if she doesn't get better?*

Chapter 24

She did get better. Three days after she was found, Gloria finally came out of the coma. Emilio was at her bedside half-reading a book, half-listening to music on his iPod, and keeping an eye on the bed where the still figure lay, when suddenly he saw her eyelids flicker.

Emilio jumped up. At once her eyes cleared. She murmured, 'Milo,' and reached for his hand.

Emilio's chest tightened with relief, with love, with feelings he couldn't name. Hanging on to her hand, he gasped, 'Oh, Mamá, I'm so glad, so glad you're awake.'

Something like fear leapt into her eyes. 'I don't remember what . . . How long have I been . . . '

Tía Isabel had told Emilio how they'd found his mother lying unconscious, tied to some rusty old pipes in a tiny airless room in the basement of the abandoned building. 'She looked like a broken rag doll,' she'd said, her eyes full of tears. 'Oh my God, Milo, it was so terrible to see her in that state.'

But he didn't want to tell his mother any of that now.

So he said, 'You've been here three days. The doctor said – said you'd been heavily dosed. He said . . . ' But he couldn't finish, his voice was too choked with emotion.

'Oh my poor Milo. My sweet brave boy,' she said, with tears in her eyes, and they hugged each other, gently, because of her bruises.

'Shall I help you sit up, Mamá?' he said after a moment, and when she said yes, he arranged the pillows behind her and helped her up. It was then that the rest of the family came back. Oh, the cries of joy that ensued then! Oh the tears and smiles and kisses and hugs! Gloria said, with a rueful twist of the mouth, 'I've been such a trouble to you all. You've all been through such a terrible time for my sake, and I'm so sorry . . . '

'Don't you dare be sorry,' ordered Isabel. 'It'll make you ill all over again and that would never do. You're not to worry about a single thing, not a thing, you understand.'

'But—'

'No buts. You're not allowed to worry until you're all better,' said her sister, kissing her on the cheek.

Emilio called his grandfather with the news that his mother was awake – he had of course been told days ago that she'd been found – and Gloria insisted on speaking to him at once. It was only a brief conversation, but Emilio could tell it was a good one, and that for the first time in years, his mother and grandfather were connecting, awkwardly perhaps, but definitely. 'He's invited us both to Mérida when I'm feeling better,' said Gloria when she hung up, 'and do you know, Milo, we might take him up on that, what do you think?'

'Oh yes,' said Emilio, his heart swelling with gladness, 'I think that is such a good idea.'

Later that morning, Señor Sellers called from Arizona, and was also delighted to hear the good news. He too spoke briefly to Gloria, and told her that as far as he was concerned, the deal with his company and hers was still very much alive. 'Bill Taylor and I have talked it over, and we can help cover things for a while and give you support,' he said, 'till you're back on your feet.'

'But you've taken a big risk on my account,' she said. 'The hotel shares—'

'Why, don't you fret about that, Gloria,' he said. 'All's just fine. Nobody's taking our hotel. It's all working out. All's well that ends well. So don't worry.'

'You are good men, both of you,' said Gloria in a shaky voice, to which he replied, 'No, ma'am, we are just businessmen and we're fully expecting that this will be to our mutual benefit,' but they all knew the truth, and were glad. The kidnap had shown the cruelty and vicious greed of some people but also the kindness and courage of others, and that afternoon, when Castro came to the hospital to interview Gloria, this was emphasised again. While the policeman was in the room with Gloria, recording her statement, Alda told the rest of the family outside that thanks to Evita's information, Esposito had been arrested, in company with a young woman whom they now knew was the so-called Flor de la Noche.

'What about Evita? ' asked Emilio anxiously. 'If they find out she gave them up . . . '

'They won't,' said Alda. 'Everything about Evita is off the record, I promise you that.'

Castro confirmed that later. 'You see, we picked them both up on a technicality, nothing to do with the interrogation, and he believed it, so now he's giving us chapter and verse. We've also now picked up two other gang members. They all swear blind it was all their idea and el Capitán Medina had nothing to do with it. They're loyal to their boss – or scared of him, or both. It's going to take some time to pin it on him as well. But we won't give up, and at least we have those four in custody.'

'What about the money, did you find that?' said Tío Vicente, earning himself a cross look from his wife.

'I'm afraid only a portion of that was recovered,' said the policeman, 'about a quarter of it, in fact. We suspect the rest of it was funnelled immediately to Medina through an intermediary, possibly a crooked lawyer, and we're looking into that too. But of course what's been recovered, which must have been the percentage for those who actually snatched Señora Lopez, will be returned to you as soon as possible. I'm sorry I don't have better news on that.'

'It doesn't matter,' said Tía Isabel. 'We can deal with that later. All that counts right now is that Gloria's safe, and with us again.'

'Yes, of course,' said Castro.

'Was Gloria able to identify Esposito and Flor and the others?' asked Juanita.

'Well, she only saw them briefly when she was first abducted – they either wore hoods or kept her blindfolded when they were with her, even when she spoke to you on the phone. So she never really saw their faces clearly, but she heard their voices and recognised them all right on the tape I played her, extracted from the interrogation I've conducted with both Flor and Esposito. They were pretty careful about using names in her presence – but they slipped up once and she overheard one of them call out to Flor, which is why she passed on that message to you. They never guessed. A quick thinker, your mother.' He smiled. 'Like mother, like son.'

Emilio flushed. He said, 'Can I – can I ask you a favour, Agent Castro?'

'Sure. What is it?' said the policeman.

'Can I please – I'd like to see – I mean, I would like to see their faces.'

'Emilio!' protested his aunt. 'Why would you want that? It'll only give you nightmares.'

'No,' said Emilio. 'It's – it's the opposite.' It was difficult to explain what was in his mind, that otherwise the faceless creatures that had haunted his life for those two terrible weeks would stay as monstrous shadows, gnawing away at him, if he didn't put faces and names to them. He wanted to explain that he needed to see them if he was ever to start to purge the poison of what had happened and begin to feel safe again. But he couldn't bring out the words.

But Alda understood. He could see that in her eyes. She said, 'Raúl, I think it can be done, don't you?'

'Yes,' said the policeman simply, and then he opened the folder he held and showed them four photographs. One was of Esposito, whom they recognised from the nightclub camera tape; two were of two other young men, one burly, with hard eyes and a sharp haircut; the other small and wiry, with a soft face. ('Your caretaker recognised that one as the courier who brought the first message, after your mother was abducted,' Castro explained to Emilio.) And the fourth was of a young woman in her early twenties, no older than Juanita or Alda. She wasn't the girl on Esposito's arm in the night-club, but someone they'd never seen before. And she was quite pretty too, a little like Alda in looks with her petite figure and shining straight bob – if it hadn't been for a dead-eyed stare. 'We strongly suspect Flor was the ring-leader on the outside,' said Castro, 'answering directly to Medina.' A pause. 'We know a little more about her now. She's not from Sinaloa or Mexico City like the others. She's from Juárez.'

Emilio looked into the stony black eyes of the girl in the photograph, the girl who looked vaguely like Alda, and he thought, both of them grew up in the same hard and violent place, but Alda is someone who tries to save lives, while Flor is someone who tries to destroy them. Yet once they'd both been innocent little children. How did that happen, that one person can grow up to be a helper and another into a killer?

Alda had said, talking of her cousin who'd joined a gang that 'When you grow up in that atmosphere, nothing is normal.' Maybe that's what had happened to Flor and

Esposito and the others, Emilio thought. Maybe once they'd been like Evita, lost children who'd drifted into crime that just got worse and worse. Or like Alda's cousin, Joaquin, they'd come from loving but troubled backgrounds. Or like Medina, they'd been from 'connected' families where crime was a well-rewarded way of life. Or even that they'd come from ordinary families, ordinary backgrounds. But who cared? He certainly didn't. He didn't want to know their stories. What mattered was what they'd done. A last spurt of white-hot hate and rage flamed in him, then died. He'd looked at their faces and now they'd no longer be shadows. Their dirty war had burst into his life and changed it forever. He wanted them to pay for what they'd done, to be in prison for a long time. But he no longer wanted to waste any emotion on them, not even hate or anger. They weren't worth it.

He handed back the folder to Castro. He looked at the policeman, and at Alda. 'Thank you for letting me see,' he said. 'And on my behalf, and that of my mother, and all our family' – here he looked at the others, who nodded – 'I want to thank you both very much for everything you've done for us.' Solemnly, he offered his hand.

'It's our job, Emilio,' replied Castro as he shook hands. Alda did likewise, then she said, 'It has been an honour to work with you all, and I cannot say too strongly how much I admire this family's steadfastness in the face of this experience. It is always a nightmare, but strong bonds such as yours help so much. Thank you, Señor and Señora Torres, for your trust in and kindness to me, and taking me into your family when I was such an unwelcome reminder of what was happening.'

'Don't mention it,' said Tío Vicente, gruffly, pumping her hand.

Tía Isabel kissed the young negotiator on both cheeks. 'You are welcome, my dear, so very welcome, any time to visit us.'

Juanita gave her a hug, saying, 'I second exactly what Mamá said. And it's been an honour to work with you.'

'And with you,' said Alda. Then she turned to Emilio and Luz. 'And may I say that your parents must be so very proud of you both, you have been so helpful and mature and brave—'

'No, that was Emilio,' said Luz, blushing in embarrassment, 'I didn't do much, not really.'

'You did too,' said Emilio cheerfully, 'so stop contradicting people, chica,' and he hugged her and then his aunt came to them and hugged them both and then Juanita and her father, and none of them noticed Alda and Castro slipping discreetly away.

Three days after that conversation, Emilio's mother was back home, with Emilio, in their own flat. Everyone helped them settle in, and Tía Isabel stayed a few extra days with them, 'just to help out', as she said, because Gloria was still a little weak from her ordeal. It was strange to be back, but good too. Señor Santiago was so pleased to see them, and so were their neighbours in the building – even people they'd hardly ever spoken to before told them how glad they were to see Gloria safe.

Emilio went back to school on the second day after his mother returned home, and though he dreaded that his friends might ply him with questions, they didn't. They were all too relieved that it had all ended well, and that his mother was safe and getting better by the day. Pablo did ask him if he wanted revenge against the kidnappers, and after a moment Emilio shrugged and said he hoped they'd go to prison for a long time, that was all, and Pablo saw the look on his face and didn't persist.

A couple of weeks after, Emilio and his mother went for a weekend to Mérida, but not alone, for the rest of the family had been invited too. It was a little stiff at first but in the end turned out very well, and on the drive back to Mexico City, Tío Vicente said, 'He's a gentleman of the old school, that one,' and Gloria said, with a little sigh, 'Yes, he is. He's a fine man.'

They'd gone together, just the three of them, Emilio, his mother and his grandfather, to his father's grave, and there Gloria and Juán had listened silently while Emilio laid some flowers at Jorge's grave and told the story of all that had happened. 'But we're all here now, Papá,' he finished, 'and we all love you, and miss you,' and when he looked up at the adults, he saw their eyes were full of tears. Tears of sadness but also of gladness, and in that moment, he knew that something had changed, and that his mother and grandfather understood something about each other at last. They'd not ever be as close to each other as Emilio was to both of them, of course. But it would do. It would do very well.

Chapter 25

It is a Sunday many months later. Emilio is back at his aunt's and uncle's place. But it's different, this time. His mother's there too, and his grandfather, and soon his friends will be arriving, Pablo and Sierra and Nina and Sergio, and so will many others, neighbours and friends of the family, for this is going to be one big party. The tables are groaning with food and drink, Luz and Juanita are buzzing around putting up decorations, his grandfather and his uncle are cheerfully arguing over music for the party, his mother and his aunt are making enough tortillas for an army, checking sauces, tossing salads. Emilio is running around helping everyone in turn, or 'getting in everyone's way', as Luz informs him when he tries to tell her that the decoration she's put up is crooked.

Emilio doesn't mind Luz telling him off. He doesn't mind anything, as long as everyone is together, safe, and things are normal again. As he rushes around, he thinks how lucky they've been. Sure, the rest of the ransom money has never been found, but the insurance companies did refund most of it, under the kidnap clause, and Emilio's grandfather recovered nearly all his money. The bank was very understanding and helped Lopez Travel through the difficult time, and as Señor Sellers had promised, the deal between Lopez Travel and Holiday South went through and was duly celebrated at the long-delayed party. As to the kidnappers, the law still ground on very slowly but eventually they were brought to trial and all convicted and sentenced to long stretches in prison. They'd steadfastly refused to give up Medina, but in the end it didn't matter – mysteriously, the gangster was found stabbed to death in the prison library one day. Though like so many killings connected with the drug war the murder was never solved, the rumour was that it was to do with a falling-out with the Sinaloa cartel. Something to do with a hotel that had been promised to them, but never materialised.

As to Evita, *I was right*, Emilio thinks. After she'd been released from hospital, she'd evaded the people who were supposed to take her to the orphanage, but in the end Padre Benitez found her. Though at first she fought against being there, in time she grew used to it and even to like it. It is a good place, quiet and small. Many of the children there have been orphaned by gang violence, and the staff are dedicated and kind, but more than that, they understand.

Evita texts and calls from time to time, and she and Emilio exchange links to cartoons and movies. He's visited her a few times too, by himself and with Luz, and one time Evita told him she'd decided that what she wants to do when she grows up is make cartoons. She showed them cartoons she drew and even a simple animation she filmed using the iPhone camera. It looked totally like something a kid had made, Emilio thought, *but that's okay. She is a kid. It's a start.*

The door-buzzer rings. Someone else has arrived, and is buzzed in by Juanita. Emilio is carrying a pile of plates to the dining room when the door opens. It's Padre Benitez and Alda, but also another person, looking much more shy than Emilio has ever seen her. 'Evita!' he says, smiling, putting the plates down and coming towards her, with Luz. 'We're so glad you could come.'

Author's note

I have followed events in Mexico for quite a while,
partly because of a personal interest in the culture of
this extraordinary country – an interest that began in
childhood when I first devoured books about the great
pre-Columbian empires of Mexico – and partly because
my son Xavier has spent long periods of time in Mexico
over the last few years. As I Skyped with Xavier over
many months (and prayed he would stay safe and would
never be in the wrong place at the wrong time!), I came
to a better understanding of what was happening in
Mexico and just how the drug war affects family life and
people's everyday experiences. Nothing is guaranteed.
Nothing can be taken for granted. It is this feeling that
underlies *Emilio* – the feeling of what happens when
a nightmare that's always hovered at the edge of your
vision suddenly becomes a lived reality.

The Mexican drug war has claimed over 60 000 lives
since 2006; in fact, some reports put the figure as high
as 100 000. The war shows no sign of letting up, despite
successive changes of government. Although Mexico has
become more prosperous recently, and in many ways
is a wonderful and exciting place with its rich, complex
culture and strong joie de vivre, the drug war has caused
deep trauma to the Mexican people. Unlike most wars,
which are often the result of tribal conflict or an invasion
by foreign forces, the Mexican drug war is both a civil war

and a war fed by foreign elements, in this case, primarily by the US drug market. It is both a conflict between rival cartels/gangs battling for supremacy, and a war between the major cartels and the Mexican government forces.

There has been armed conflict over drugs for decades in Mexico, particularly in the north, but a more generalised civil war began after a government crackdown in 2006. The cartels assumed control of the trade formerly organised by the Colombian cartels. It's a brutal business – they vie with each other in atrocities and the public display of dismembered bodies. As well as the high death toll among gang members, government forces, police, journalists, politicians and priests, there have been many thousands of ordinary people injured and tortured, thousands of children orphaned and many people reported missing. Whole communities are living in fear and the annual rate of kidnappings continues to be alarming.

Meanwhile, corruption within the system, particularly within the police force, all too often allows criminals to continue their reign of terror. Corruption isn't just about money, it is also about fear, and many police officers are simply too scared to do anything more than keep their heads down. This is one of the reasons why new federal police services, backed by the army, were created.

A recent development, in some states, is the formation of armed vigilante groups that claim they can protect communities from the violence of the cartels by directly confronting them and also by disarming the local police, who they say are in league with the cartels. Such a development is an indication of how little faith desperate people have in the police, and in fact the government has as much as admitted it by allowing the groups to operate now as 'Rural Defence Forces'. But it must also be said that there are many dedicated police officers who risk their lives every day trying to protect the community.

Children and young people have been directly involved in this pitiless war as relatives of murder and kidnap victims, or as victims themselves. Some are also perpetrators; there are increasing numbers of brutal-ised child and teenage assassins who often commit their lucrative crimes while high on the drugs the cartels give them. On the other hand, some young people attempt to make a difference, either by direct confrontation in vigilante groups – whose members are often young men in their late teens and early twenties – or in other less violent ways. One notable example is the nineteen-year-old woman who became a police chief in a district where no one else would take the position. (Alas, after only a year she had to quit her job and flee to the US for asylum.) Then there are the teenagers who joined an extraordinary movement called 'the Messengers'; they stand on street corners dressed in angel costumes, holding up signs appealing to kidnappers and hitmen to repent. The harsh reality is that no one is entirely out of reach of this terrible war.

Timeline

1980 Miguel Angel Félix Gallardo founds Guadalajara Cartel, first cartel to prosper from Colombian cocaine trade. Guadalajara controls illegal drug trade across Mexico–US border.

1980s Gallardo divides trade among top drug leaders. Sinoloa and Tijuana cartels created following his arrest in 1989.

1990-2000 Violence escalates between the major cartels: Los Zetas, Sinaloa, Gulf, Tijuana and Juárez.

2001 Joaquín Guzmán Loera, 'El Chapo', escapes from federal prison vows to take control of Mexico's drug trade with his Sinaloa Cartel.

2005 Guzmán breaks non-aggression pact of the major cartels with the assassination of Juárez Cartel leader. Violence escalates across Mexico, about 15 000 people killed.

2006 Operation Michoacán President Felipe Calderón launches first government offensive against drug cartels. Estimated 6500 Mexican military deployed to Michoacán, capturing La Familia leader and killing 500 cartel members.

2007 More than 20 000 Mexican soldiers and federal police deployed across Mexico. Almost 3000 people killed and an estimated 284 federal police commanders dismissed. US President George W. Bush pledges $1.4 billion in drug-fighting gear and training for Mexico and Central America.

2008 Inter-cartel disputes continue as Guzmán takes on the Juárez Cartel near Ciudad Juárez – the drug war's bloodiest flashpoint with over 6000 deaths. Cartels diversify into kidnapping, human trafficking and extortion.

2009 President Calderón sends 10 000 troops to Ciudad Juárez. Violence spreads to Arizona. US President Barack Obama vows to end gun-smuggling into Mexico as drug-war death toll soars above 9000. Braullo Arellano Domínguez, leader of Loz Zetas Cartel, is killed in gun battle with Mexican forces.

2010 Gulf Cartel leader, Osiel Cárdenas Gullén, sentenced to twenty-five years in Texan prison. Worsening police corruption results in dismissal of more than 3000 officers. Los Zetas Cartel kidnaps and kills 72 South and Central American migrants in Tamaulipas for refusing to traffic drugs. Ciudad Juárez becomes Mexico's most violent city.

2011 Mexico's military captures 11 544 people linked to cartels and organised crime. US Senate report reveals 70 per cent of guns recovered from Mexican crime scenes were sourced in US. Several mass graves holding 177 bodies are discovered in Tamaulipas, taking the estimated death toll to 43 000.

2012 President Calderón's offensive results in the deaths of more than 40 major cartel members but causes the splintering of cartels into more extreme rival organisations.

    Mexico City becomes new target, with Mano con Ojos group claiming responsibility for severed heads found in the city.

2012 Mexican President Enrique Peña Nieto takes office and vows to reduce crime and violence as cartels engage in more terrorist acts, focusing on public servants such as city mayors. An estimated 30 000 Mexican children are involved in organised crime.

2013 Human Rights Watch report estimates more than 60 000 people killed and about 10 000 missing due to drug-related violence. US Treasury declares 'El Chapo' the most influential trafficker in the world, his milti-billion dollar enterprise stretching to 54 countries. Record year for kidnappings in Mexico, with 1583 reported incidents.

2014 The rise of vigilante militia in Michoacán and Guerrero and other areas with high kidnapping rates creates a third force in Mexico's drug war. Guzmán captured in Maxatlán, Sinaloa by Mexican and US security forces.

Glossary

abuelo grandfather
albondiga meatballs
agua fresco a drink made from fruit juices, such as
mango and watermelon
arroz con pollo rice with chicken
bastardos bastards
café con crème coffee with cream
caldo de pollo chicken soup
caldo de res a hearty beef soup
cantina pub
Carlos Slim A Mexican business magnate, investor
and philanthropist, once ranked the richest person
in the world
chica girl
chilli quesos cheesy, spicy dip eaten with fresh
tortillas
chiquita little girl
churros a Spanish doughnut
cielito literally 'little heaven'; or darling
corazoncito mio my little heart
Día de los Inocentes Day of the Innocents
(in memory of children who have died)
Día de los Muertos Day of the Dead
empanadas a savoury fried pastry filled with meat
Federales a slang name for the Policía Federal or
Federal Police ('the Feds')
flan con nata crème caramel with whipped cream
hermana sister

hermano   brother

hombre   man

Maestra   Teacher

mariachi   a traditional dance music very popular in Mexico, featuring bands playing stringed instruments such as guitars and violins, and trumpets

mi amor   my love

mi hermana querida   my darling sister

muy delicioso   very delicious

pendejos   rotten bastard

Policía Federal   Federal Police; see also Federales

telenovela   soap opera

tonto   idiot

tres leches   three milks (tres leches cake is made with whole milk, condensed milk and evaporated milk)

Find out more about...

Mexico

http://news.bbc.co.uk/2/hi/americas/country_
profiles/1205074.stm

http://www.bbc.co.uk/news/world-latin-
america-18095241

http://www.youtube.com/watch?v=nrHtTmBNc6c
(fast-forward through the opening advertisement)

Brownlie, Bojang, Ali. *Mexico*, Raintree, London, 2012

Peppas, Lynn. *Cultural traditions in Mexico*, Crabtree
Publishing Company, New York, 2012

Mexico's Drug War

http://www.bbc.co.uk/news/world-latin-
america-10681249

http://edition.cnn.com/2013/09/02/world/americas/
mexico-drug-war-fast-facts/

http://www.youtube.com/watch?v=pLlrbAZv9Do

http://edition.cnn.com/2012/01/17/world/americas/
mexico-city-security/

http://www.mcclatchydc.com/2013/10/31/207103/
kidnappings-soar-in-mexico-with.html

Effects of Drug War on children in Mexico

http://www.npr.org/2012/11/27/166027034/mexicos-
drug-war-is-changing-childhood

http://news.nationalpost.com/2011/07/19/mexican-
drug-war-claiming-more-child-victims/

Acknowledgements

This is a work of fiction, but I've used many sources for research, including news reports on the ever-evolving situation in Mexico, as well as the books listed below. My thanks to Xavier Masson-Leach and J.L. Powers for helpful advice on Mexican daily life and culture.

Campbell, Howard. *Drug War Zone: Frontline Dispatches from the Streets of El Paso and Juárez*, University of Texas Press, Austin, 2009
This book, which mainly consists of a series of interviews, is notable in that it presents the personal words and experiences of the 'narcos', the drug dealers, and also those of people on the other side, the police and other law enforcers. It gives great insights into how the cartels operate, too, and how they have taken hold.

Gibler, John. *To Die in Mexico: Dispatches from Inside the Drug War*, City Lights Publishers, San Francisco, 2011
This American journalist decided to visit some of Mexico's most dangerous towns and neighbourhoods in order to bring back first-hand reports and interviews with people on all sides of the drug war. He profiles the corruption that enables the drug cartels to get so rich and powerful, and also focuses on the courageous – and dangerous – role that journalists have played in covering

the war. His solution, to legalise drugs, won't however meet with everyone's approval.

Valseca, Jayne Garcia with Mark Ebner. *We Have Your Husband: One Woman's Terrifying Story of a Kidnapping in Mexico*, Berkley, New York, 2011
This is a chilling account of a terrifying, months-long ordeal in which Mexican newspaper publisher Eduardo Valseca Garcia was held by a kidnap gang, while his American wife Jayne attempted to deal with the kidnappers' ever-increasing demands, with the help of a young negotiator from the Federales. This book was very important in my research, as it described in detail an evolving kidnap situation, and how kidnaps are dealt with in Mexico. It has also been made into a movie.

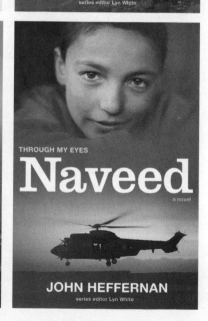